"Particularly poignant is Belgrave's depiction of Louise's guilt and sorrow at having to end unintended pregnancies with uncaring lovers, contrasting with her later desire, unfulfilled, to get pregnant when she is able at last to find steady, true love. Belgrave's tale reveals life for poverty-stricken citizens of a picturesque island that seems like paradise for those who come only for short sojourns."

—Reviewed by Barbara Bamberger Scott – Premium US Reviewers

Growing Up in Barbados

Growing Up in Barbados

Sereta Belgrave

Library of Congress Control Number: 2013901553
ISBN: Hardcover   978-1-4797-8613-8
                     Softcover   978-1-4797-8612-1
                     eBook   978-1-4797-8614-5

Print information available on the last page.

Rev. date: 12/19/2018

To order additional copies of this book, contact:
Xlibris
1-888-795-4274
www.Xlibris.com
Orders@Xlibris.com
600360

I dedicate this book to my two beloved children, Sean and Ross, both of whom have been an inspiration.

Dear reader,

M OST OF US will agree that the socialization process as a child is pivotal to the personalities we develop and the person we ultimately become later in life. Some of us, in spite of the odds, can and do overcome inadequate social or intellectual behavior, which was as a result of imperfect development, both tangible and intangible. For some, the change may occur early in life, if given the opportunity to do so. Most of us probably know of at least one situation where there was a complete turnaround in attitude and behavior in a relatively short period of time. In other circumstances, the downward spiral may continue and could lead to a very destructive and wasted life.

I am a romantic at heart and do believe that there is a brighter tomorrow and that, if given a chance, an individual can truly be successful in spite of obstacles they have encountered early in life during the socialization process. Was Louise, the main character of this novel, with its setting in the beautiful and idyllic island of Barbados, which is located in the Caribbean, successful, having experienced some of the worst situations life has to offer? Of course, it ultimately depends on how you measure success!

My degree from the University of the West Indies–Cave Hill Campus, Barbados, is in the social sciences specifically a bachelor of science in management studies. However, deep within me there has always been the desire to gravitate toward the humanities as I am a people's person. I have learned that my interest in people in general and the various situations that can and do occur can truly be demonstrated and accomplished through writing.

This is my first novel, but I can assure you that it will not be the last. I hope you enjoyed this book as much as I have enjoyed writing it.

Regards,
Sereta Belgrave

Chapter 1

I T WAS EARLY morning in late February. The weather was picture perfect, brilliant sunshine, clear blue sky, but very light winds. Naomi and her co-worker Mildred were already in the sugar cane fields at the sugar plantation where they work in Christ Church, Barbados, cutting canes. Naomi turned to Mildred, while she wiped the sweat from her face with the apron she wore, "Mildred! I don't know about you, but it is very warm already." Mildred responded, "Oh yes it is very hot indeed." They both continued with the cutting of canes; and placed them in heaps for loading on to the tractor later in the evening. The tractor subsequently takes them to the factory where they would be converted to cane sugar.

Barbados is a mere 167 square miles and is the most easterly of the Caribbean island chain. The Portuguese explorer Pedro a Campos discovered Barbados in 1536 while in route to Brazil. He called it Los Barbados (the bearded ones) allegedly after the island's fig trees; whose long hanging aerial roots have a bearded-like resemblance. Unlike most of the other islands in the Caribbean, Barbados is very flat, and it rises gradually from the sea on the West Coast to its highest point, Mount Hillaby, in the parish of Saint Andrew, which is over one thousand feet above sea level. Barbados is divided into eleven parishes. Its formation is mainly of coral and limestone. The majority of its inhabitants are of African descent. It has an African population of approximately 90 percent and a white population of approximately 4 percent, with the remaining population mainly of Asian/mixed descent.

Barbados was settled into by the English colonists from 1627. Until the abolition of slavery in the British Empire in 1834, most of the slaves came from Africa to work on the sugar plantations. It remained a colony of Britain until it attained internal autonomy in 1961. In 1966 it became an independent nation but remained part of the Commonwealth. The official language is English. However most Barbadians also speak 'Bajan' dialect. It is a fun way to speak, but when it becomes an impediment to the point where a Barbadian cannot converse in standard English when required to do so, then there is the problem.

As it approached midday, Naomi said to Mildred "This sweltering heat is just too much to bare sometimes." Mildred responded, "You got that right." Naomi stopped momentarily with right hand on hip, while wiping the sweat from her face, said to Mildred, "I don't know about you, but I had this dream that one day the plantation overseer Charles Marshall will really 'take me on' and get me out of this predicament of cutting canes day in and day out in this sweltering heat." Mildred responded and said "I feel Mr. Marshall would take you on, and yes he may even want to have sex with you too. I always see him eying your broad backside and your big boobs. Besides, you know these British white men, they have an eye for we black women with those two assets."

Mildred suddenly came closer to Naomi, "Hear this, one of the other women who recently start to work with us cutting canes told me that Mr. Marshall even slapped 'she' on her backside already and brush against her breasts." Naomi looked alarmed, stepped back, and with a very expressive and intense look on her face said, "Wait, and what did she do?" "What she do like what.", said Mildred, "She was so glad to see that he like he wanted to have sex with her of all of we plantation laborers that she just went along and gave him a big broad smile, hoping that it would happen again. Who knows maybe he would eventually tell her that he coming for 'some', and I believe she would oblige him too. You know that we black women 'does' feel very proud to have a white overseer looking at us and if we could get more attention and action that would be even better." Mildred chuckled, and said, "So you might be lucky too."

Naomi giggled like a school girl, then she said, "That would be so nice, Lord Oh Lord. Let it be. I have to admit that I fall into the category of wanting attention from a white man, especially one who has a 'big up' job like him." Mildred responded and said, "strange how these British plantation overseers have no problem taking we black women who are well endowed, especially when we still hot and sweaty, after a long day's work in the field, that like it is a great turn on for them."

Naomi looked up in the air as if in deep thought said "I have an idea." "What?" asked Mildred? Naomi with excitement in her voice said "The next time he comes close to me, I am going to give him a big broad smile, maybe even broader if possible than that woman you talked about. I mean a real come on look, and also make sure he gets to touch me too, maybe even 'feel me up', if nobody is around."

They both had a good laugh. Suddenly with a serious look on her face Naomi said, "But between you and me, I would not want it to be a one-time thing, I would want it to continue because I feel materially I would benefit." And then as if in a trance said, "Just thinking about 'he' on top of me having sex with me is a great turn on. You would not believe it, but my body is beginning to tingle already."

Mildred looked at Naomi intently then said to her, "Well girl, I would be happy for you, but those people still have their racists biases. He will happily get on top of you and for sure give you the rough sex too, but material benefits; to be honest I don't know about that." They continued with their day's work in the cane field. Around 1:00 p.m. they stopped to have their lunch which they each kept in a flask to keep warm. They removed their aprons, placed them on the ground and sat on top of them to protect their backside from the sweltering heat while they continued to chat on the same subject. Naomi said to Mildred, "Getting back to our conversation, I think you are right, Ma (Naomi's mother) always say how racists these people are. They show you a nice face and a charming smile but underneath they feel that we black women are just a piece of meat, or maybe even garbage, just to be used and disposed of after. Funny how they think so little of us, but still want to have sex with us."

Mildred responded, "That is so true. As my son who is more educated than me would say such a contra... I think the word is contradiction; but Naomi I know you are so in awe of Mr. Marshall that you even get turn on when you see him approaching. I know because I 'does' eye you to get your reaction." Naomi with her head looking downward said "You are so right, but I would want him for 'keeps' like I said before not a one-time thing. I guess it may never become a reality, based on the way this Barbadian society place all of us in categories, depending on our job, and color and me just a poor laborer." She raised her head said, "But I guess there is nothing wrong in my dreaming of a better life one day with a man like Mr. Marshall, and getting out of the sugar cane fields."

Mildred with a serious look on her face said "Agreed. But realistically, as the saying goes, you might live in hope but die in desperation."

Naomi looked dejected said, "But we are such great friends, please build me up. Don't pull me down any further; you know I do not have much confidence in myself. Besides, I prefer to make believe of a better life even if it remains a dream." She continued in a very expressive tone, "and Mildred I like Mr. Marshall real bad though. Between you and me, every night when I go home, he is the last person I think about, thinking mostly that he is on top of me having some sweet sex before drifting off." Mildred shook her head said, "I am loss for words. I really don't know what to tell you."

It was now 4:00 p.m. They completed their work by placing the canes in proper heaps for loading the next morning on to trailers which are attached to tractors to be transported to the sugar factory. They then proceeded on their separate way home.

Naomi continued to dream of a better life, but a better life was not to be. She remained in the sugar cane fields, has five children, all from five different men.

The next morning Naomi's mother Lillian visited her. She stood up outside of the small run down chattel house that her daughter occupied and greeted each of her grandchildren who took turns appearing at the small window. After the greet, in a very serious tone of voice, Lillian said to Naomi, "What happen to you though, these five children that you have are more than enough, every time I look around you breeding again, the same thing that happened to me now happening to you. She raised her voice shouting said, "Don't lie down and get any more. Life is too hard in this country Barbados." The cycle which started with Naomi's grandmother, then her own mother Lillian continued to be very pervasive, now she with the same fate.

The opportunity came for Naomi to finally 'Make Out', with Mr. Marshall, the Plantation Overseer. It was just after 5:30 p.m., after a hard day's work in the sugar cane fields Naomi found a bunch of keys. With the sweat still pouring down her face, her back and under her arm pit, she instantly knew that the only person that they could belong too was Mr. Marshall. She walked to his office, knocked on his door. Mr. Marshall appeared at the door. She said, "Good evening Sir, I just found these keys on my way in from the sugar cane fields. Do they belong to you Sir?"

He beckoned her to come in, proceeded to lock the door behind her. In a surprise tone of voice he said "Oh yes, they are. Gosh. I searched everywhere for them. Thank you so very much." He then paused for a minute, looked her up and down and with excitement in his voice said, "And how was your day?" She now in awe of her heart throb so close to her nervously said, "Lots of hard work as usual Sir, but I don't mine. I love my work."

Mr. Marshall moved closer to her in the already small office space while gazing down at her voluptuous breasts and salivating said, "mmmmm I can see that you sweaty all over." He proceeded to touch her face, and then his hands moved down to other parts of her body in a sensual way which included her neck and breasts. Suddenly, he grabbed hold of her, pushed her down on the desk while telling her, "You are so sweaty and nice all over mmmmmmmmm but what is your name again?" Before she could say her name with clarity, he with intense excitement raised her skirt, then raised her feet up in the air, and said, "Oh I remember the name now, Naomi right. Do you know how I remember? The backside and the voluptuous breasts."

She gave him a broad smile and giggled like a school girl. He unbuttoned her blouse pushing her bra up, exposing her huge sweaty breasts. He hurriedly unzipped his pants, pushed her underwear to one side, and had some very rough sex with her. In less than two minutes he was done. With a broad smile on his face, he uttered, "Good Job. That was so nice, you were sweaty in the right places, and that was a huge turn on for me." However, his demeanor quickly changed. In a serious tone of voice, he opened the door and said to her, "You may leave now."

She should have been upset with regard to his haste to get her out of his office, but appeared quite calm and collected, said nothing to anyone about her sexual encounter. Too herself aloud with a smile on her face said, *"Lord I feel like I am dreaming, that was short and rough but sweet."*

Just over six weeks later, while cutting and loading canes in the sugar cane fields, Naomi said to Mildred, "I did not say anything to you, but I missed my period, and I feeling like I want to vomit in the morning every day. I like I 'gone cross'." Mildred abruptly stopped working, one hand on the right hip said in a surprised tone of voice and expression on her face, "'Gone cross, but I was saying to myself that you looking very fat and your breasts look even bigger than usual. I thought you told me that you finish with that. I mean with sex, and how you don't want any man, because you already have five children from five different men. What happen there now?" Naomi hesitated for a moment, responded, "But Mildred, this one is different. I am happy and sad at the same time. You are not going to believe that what I wish for happened, but I did not expect it would happen so soon and that it would be more than sex." Mildred tilted her head back ward and in an extremely surprised tone of voice said, "What are you talking about? You mean to tell me, you gave Mr. Marshall 'some'."

Naomi with head down said, "Yes I did," Then quickly added, "No. No. Actually I did not give him, he 'take' it. It happened so fast that I only realize it happen after it was done. I 'did' like it very much though, but now I don't know what to do." Mildred responded, "What to do like what? You better go and explain that to Mr. Marshall. You should have told him ever since, once you know that he is the only one." Naomi very expressive said, "Of course he is. I told you that I finish with men." With a faint smile on her face she said, "Another thing, the same thing we discussed, I was real sweaty, and that really turned him on, and he was very rough, but sweet."

Sarcastically, Mildred responded and said, "Oh yes, he was sweet. Anyway, the sooner you talk to him the better." Naomi lowered her head again as she reflected on the entire episode and said, "Okay I will, I am a bit nervous, but I will tell you how it work out." Mildred became very agitated and demonstrative said, "Nervous. Go and get it off your 'chest', and go along fast, do what I tell you."

The following morning at exactly 7:30 a.m. though nervous Naomi knocked on Mr. Marshall's office door. Mr. Marshall opened the door half way and remained there, with a very serious look on his face. He said too her, "I understand you want to discuss something with me." She responded, "Yes Sir I do. He beckoned her to come in. He became impatient and in a formal tone said "Have a seat," then quickly said "What is it that you want to talk to me about. I am very busy today and do not have much time to talk to you." She said to herself, *"He wasn't too busy when he was on top of me six weeks ago."*

She became extremely nervous, said to him "I have discovered that after our encounter the other day, about six weeks ago... He appeared nonchalant. She hesitated momentarily, and then continued. "Remember when I found your keys, well to make a long story short, I am now 'with child' for you, because I have not had my period and I am feeling a little 'sicky'. 'sicky' most mornings, so we have to talk." Mr. Marshall's face turned 'red' with anger and disdain, said to her, "Oh, we do. I don't know about that. How do I know it 'don't' belong to one of your several men?" She was in a state of shock, surprise and agitated at the same time said, "You make me feel so special that day, now you are in denial. That is not right and you know that too. You are the only man that I went with, so unless I am like the Virgin Mary, it would have to be your child."

Mr. Marshall raised his voice while looking at her belly bump said, "Listen to me. If you are indeed pregnant for me, you should kill it. Let's be realistic, you know that my family would never ever accept that bastard you are carrying into our household."

Naomi got up from the chair where she sat and in his face with anger and hurt at the same time said, "Are you for real?" He stood up very erect, opened the door and gestured with right hand said to her, "Listen to me, go, go jump up in the air, and jump up real hard. If you try long enough you will have a miscarriage and you will not even have to go through the pain of child labor. Furthermore, I would not have to find the money for you to have an illegal abortion. Just go. Do as I say." She, stunned at his reaction burst into tears, bawling while holding her belly, said, "Lord have mercy! Just so. Never in my dreams would I have believed that you are so uncaring. You raped me that evening and dump me right away. It's like to you I am an abandoned stray dog." He became livid and said, "Just leave and leave fast. Now! Because if you do not I will have to make a report of harassment. And besides, no one will ever believe you if you tell them I breed you. Furthermore, stop keeping all of that noise in here, and for that matter outside of my office too. Save that for your rundown shack."

She departed as instructed, still crying but muffled, in response to his request that she should stop keeping so much noise. A short distance away from his office she became so overwhelmed with what had transpired, she dropped to the ground and curled up in a fetal position started bawling again. A tractor driver heard the sound, turned in the direction of the sound, saw her, ran over to her and bending over her he asked, "What happen, did someone trouble you? Do you want me to help you?" Naomi shook her head in the affirmative, still crying but softer. She responded to him said, "I will be alright. Thanks, but just do me a favor, go to the office and tell the overseer Mr. Marshall that I am feeling sick and excuse me from work for the remainder of the day." He said to her, "Sure I will do so right away."

The tractor driver ran in the direction of the Overseer's office to convey the message. She 'pulled' herself together and wiped away her tears using her apron. Shortly thereafter still extremely stressed and in a state of shock she proceeded on her journey home.

Meanwhile Mr. Marshall suddenly departed Barbados on his way to his native country England just before the birth of her baby.

Two days later, the Book Keeper summoned all of the plantation workers to a meeting. It was held outside of the Overseer's office. He informed them of the departure of Mr. Marshall. He said, "I have been asked to advise everyone that Mr. Marshall, the Overseer had an emergency and returned to England unexpectedly. His absence will not alter the conditions of your work in any way, and everyone is expected to give of their best. There will be a replacement shortly."

Some of the workers appeared shocked and verbally said that he is a nice man and wondered what could have gone wrong. They hoped that he would be okay. Others said that he should have gone back to England a long time ago, as he is not a nice person. They became very boisterous and continued giving their varying opinions. The Book Keeper in a stern voice said, "Quiet now all of you. Don't let me have to repeat myself, get back to your post immediately."

Approximately seven and a half months later, Naomi's daughter, fathered by the plantation Overseer came into the world. She immediately named her Louise. The next day Lillian, Naomi's mother visited. She held the baby, and was very surprise. She stared at the baby intently, and then in a stern tone of voice said, "Lord have Mercy! This child is mulatto." "You at twenty five, with six children now, all from six different men. I talked to you some months ago about this constant breeding, what is the matter with you?" She paused, then said loudly, "But who is 'she' father?" Naomi did not respond to the question.

Mildred visited Naomi one week later. She said to her, "everyone in this village talking about your beautiful last child. They wanted to know where you get this pretty mulatto child from, but I am not telling anybody anything." Naomi said, "Thanks I do appreciate that. These people in this village are too malicious." Then with a sad look on her face as if in despair and tears settled in her eyes said, "That announcement about her father's departure before she was born had me in a state of shock. Imagine how he picked up and left. The same thing you and I talked about. These white men on the plantation, they just want to get on top of we black women, have sex with us and then dump us like garbage. I still have not gotten over how he chased me out of his office when I told him that I am pregnant with his child. None of my other children fathers, even though they breed me and left me after were never so unkind to me."

Mildred gave her a hug, said, "I knew you were very attracted to him, but I did not know that he would get on top of you so fast, just like that and breed you. Anyway it happened already and you have your beautiful girl child. You are a good person, and the Lord is going to help you."

Naomi's brood included Oswald, the oldest; Peter, Fred, Lizzy, Avonda and Louise. Wiping the tears from her eyes she said to Mildred, "I hope my six children have a better life than me when they grow up. I would love to get out of the sugar cane fields, get a better job and get somewhere in life for my children sake." Mildred patted her on the back affectionately, said, "Pray! That is the answer." One day while Naomi was giving Louise at two years old a bath in their kitchen area, she looked intently at Louise, said to herself, *"Such a beautiful child, but Oh my God! I am a total failure. I will never let her know how she was conceived and by who. I blame myself for going to her father's office that day; I should have left the keys right where they were. Such a horrible man."*

Chapter 2

THE YEAR WAS 1955. Louise had just turned three years old. The date, to be precise, was September 22, 1955. Times were really hard back then for Louise and her family. They lived in a one-bedroom dilapidated house with a tiny area for eating, which was called the shed roof, and a kitchen, which consisted of a dirt floor. The majority of the few windows and doors were rotten, and very frequently, the rodents would enter the house from the cracks in the structure. Naomi, Louise's mother, slept on the only mattress, which was made of dried grass, usually with her male partner at that particular point in time, but all the children mostly slept on the floor.

The evening before the approach of a hurricane, which was September 21, 1955, a warning was given by a mobile van throughout the village that there was an approaching hurricane and that this system was to the south of the island. Very bad weather conditions were imminent.

In the early hours of the morning of September 22, 1955, the bells of the village church rang out, and Louise's mother, awakened all her children. She explained to them that it could be very bad and dangerous for them and they would more than likely have to seek refuge elsewhere at some point in time, alluding to the bad condition of the structure of their home and of the deteriorating weather.

Louise and her siblings were all terrified as the weather conditions deteriorated rapidly. Naomi and her children remained in the shack they called home until suddenly they heard a loud screeching noise. Naomi shouted to all her children, "get up and run, run! The house is falling down." Within minutes of their escape, the entire structure had fallen and was no more. Naomi held on tightly to Louise while urging the others to keep running. Louise started to scream, "Mother, what is going to happen to us, are we going to die?" Naomi, in a trembling voice, responded, "No, Louise, my dear child, God is going to take care of all of us."

Louise vaguely remembered the entire family running into the neighbor's house, which was still standing, to seek shelter; meanwhile, the wind was pounding. That structure was in a very dilapidated condition and as a result did not look as if it could be relied upon. Suddenly, a wind gust came with such intensity that it shattered the glass door, thus exposing everyone to the elements. Of course, with that exposure, almost instantaneously, there was a loud thundering noise.

Naomi shouted, "Come, you all, come! Let 'we' get out of here, let 'we' run, let 'we' run! Naomi had no idea where she was going but knew she had to seek shelter elsewhere for her and her brood. Meanwhile, the wind speed just would not let up and was becoming too much for Naomi and her family. Breathless but still running, clinging on to Louise, Naomi shouted, "I do not know where we are going, children, just run." Louise started to scream again and said to her mother, "Mother lift me up, I am scared. Look! Look at the sheep and dogs floating in the water. Are they going to die? Naomi knew at that point that the animals were already dead. She lifted Louise up, and covered Louise's eyes with one hand. However, while she comforted Louise, she had to place her back on the ground, clinging on to her, as running with Louise in her arms became difficult. Naomi continued to run with her children while dodging various flying objects like galvanized sheets and other debris. They ran and ran until they reached the village church. By then, Naomi and the children were out of breath; Naomi slipped and fell at the entrance, but quickly got up. She managed to mumble, "Thank God, me and my children safe now." There was tremendous overcrowding in the tiny church.

Dozens of other people from the village and surrounding districts had already arrived, most women and children and they were mostly in a panicked and very apprehensive state. Others, including the superintendent of the church, Mack, were trying to remain as calm as possible. There was a brief lull, then suddenly, as if from nowhere, the wind speed picked up again, with even more intensity than before. Within minutes, a portion of the concrete structure of the church collapsed, including the bell that previously stood majestically, that too came crashing down. Naomi, like any good mother, started to pray again, "Lord, please help me and my children to get out of this alive. Please, God, I don't want them to go down like this." Louise and other children present started to scream, some becoming hysterical and having to be consoled. The high winds and rain continued unabated. The wind speed was sustained for what appeared to be a number of hours. A while after, as the fury of nature would have it, the superintendent of the church, through a loudspeaker, suddenly said to all with much panic and anticipation in his voice, "We have to get out of here. Run! The entire structure is falling down. Just keep running."

To Naomi, it appeared like the end of the world. She jumped up, urging her children, saying, "Follow me! Follow me." There was much pandemonium. It was like hell on earth! Naomi did not look back after ensuring that all her brood was with her. Meanwhile, there was a virtual stampede. Some people were being trampled on as everyone tried to escape nature's fury literally at the same time. Naomi knew if she and the children were to come out of this terrifying experience alive, she had to think quickly as to her next move, which was where could she go now with her children. She started to pray again. "Lord God," she said, "Where can I run to now with my children?" It soon became visible to her that the majority of the houses in the village had now fallen. Those that had not collapsed entirely were without a roof. Naomi continued running frantically and aimlessly with her brood, not knowing where she was going, with dangerous objects still flying everywhere and she and the children having to duck them. She kept on running while telling her children in a trembling voice, "Don't give up, I will keep praying for us."

Suddenly and miraculously, there was calm. It was like God had answered her prayers, but Naomi was still so overwhelmed with all that was happening that she kept on running momentarily.

As if God was still on their side, Naomi met up with Dave. Dave was related to Louise's father. Of course, Naomi did not explain the connection to any of her children.

Dave was able to grant them safe haven in his family home, which was the only house that remained standing in the surrounding district. There was tremendous overcrowding in the home. Several people had sought refuge there. Dave, however, provided Naomi and the family with dry sheets and a few pillows but told them that they would have to sleep on the floor like everyone else and that his sister would not take kindly to allowing them in the vacant bedroom. Of course, Naomi felt dejected but softly said to him, "Thank you, Dave."

By late afternoon, there was total calm. As night fell upon them, Louise remembered snuggling closer and closer to her mom, wishing that Dave was her dad and that he would remove her from the hard wooden floor and allow them in the room he said that they could not use.

During the night, much confusion erupted. The sheets and pillows that Dave had given to Naomi and her family were literally dragged from beneath them by bullies who despite the bad situation even made it worse. Louise cried silently through the night but, at some point fell asleep on the hard floor from mere exhaustion. So too did her mother and siblings.

The next day, Naomi learned from Dave of the utter destruction in the surrounding areas as the eye of the hurricane, which was named Janet, had passed an estimated fifteen miles to the south of the island. Dave told her that they were very lucky as the majority of the tragedy from the hurricane took place a few miles from where she lived; which was in Oistins in the parish of Christ Church. He told her that the collapsed church where she sought shelter with the children resulted in some fatalities.

Other information he provided was that unofficial estimates gave the number of people who were left homeless at approximately twenty thousand. Of course, Naomi was part of that statistic, with an estimated 8,000 chattel houses and over 190 wall houses destroyed or seriously damaged.

Harder times now emerged for most people including Naomi and her family. Much of the population had to line up for food and other supplies, which were distributed by the government.

Louise tagged along with her mother, holding on to her mother's skirt during the lineup for food. Again, her emotions took the better of her, and she again wished that Dave was her dad. At that tender age, Louise again wondered, *but who is my dad?* Unwittingly, mixed emotions engulfed her thought process. Her hatred for her father, whoever he was overwhelmed her. Louise then figured out, *but all men are bad creatures. If my dad was not bad, he would be here to help us all. And if my sisters' and brothers' dads were not bad, they would be here to help us all.*

It was several months before Naomi, with a little assistance from the government, was able to reconstruct a small chattel house on the tenantry land she previously occupied.

It must be noted that the Barbadian chattel house is distinctive to Barbados. History shows that the Barbadian chattel house came about as a response to the distinctive events of emancipation. "The Located Laborers Act of 1840 saw the creation of new living spaces for the ex-slaves and their families on the perimeters of plantations, which became known as tenantries."

Due to the fact that the land that the former slaves occupied was rented and there was no security of tenure as such, they could be evicted for any reason or no reason. The structures had to be movable, thus the use of the word chattel. It was not unusual to see chattel houses being removed at short notice, in some cases still intact; others carefully dismantled and carried by a lorry or similar vehicle to another location. It follows that all the chattel houses on temporary rented land were also on makeshift foundations. The Bajan chattel house even at that time was attractively designed; though tiny by most standards, it had the basic tenets of Palladian/ Georgian architecture.

Foot Note: Author – Karl Watson in his book BARBADOS FIRST- The Years of Change 1920 to 1970 (Page 169) "Evolution of 'The Chattle House of Barbados"

Chapter 3

NAOMI'S SMALL CHATTEL house, though an upgrade from the one destroyed by Hurricane Janet, was still grossly inadequate for her and the children, especially the shed roof, which is known by most today as the dining area and the kitchen, which appeared to be a makeshift structure. Naomi was, however, upbeat as the children now had a shelter that they could call home again. One day shortly after moving in her new home and while preparing some cou-cou and flying fish, which is a traditional Bajan dish, for her family, Naomi was very upbeat. She asked the children, with a broad smile on her face, "Are you all happy, children?" They all, practically chanting, responded, "Yes, Mother, we are very happy." Naomi responded "Great! God is good, and tomorrow, I will prepare some good old 'Bajan' fish cakes and bakes for breakfast. And for dinner! Well, for dinner—money tight, but I know what I will prepare—I will cook some stew potatoes with some cocoa drops, how about that? Everyone chimed in, "Yes, mother, you are the best."

Naomi was very happy now that some kind of normalcy had emerged with the reconstruction of a home. No matter how humble, it was their home.

Naomi also knew that it was only a matter of time when she would have to go back to the sugar cane fields and work so that she could continue to provide basic food for her family. Naomi hated toiling in the sweltering heat cutting the canes and helping with the loading onto the trucks. Suddenly an idea came to her head. *What if I could work in the sugar cane fields a bit longer, accumulate some coppers (money), and then work as a hawker selling sugar cakes and sweets?* The more she thought about it, the more excited she became. Naomi said to herself, *Good-for-nothing Beresford* (the man that Naomi was currently involved with), *if only he would help me with more money instead of more sex, I would be able to jump-start the process.* Naomi pondered, with her thoughts about all the men in her life who fathered her six children. *All of them only wanted sex, stupid me! I always realize it when it is too late and I have another mouth to feed.* She thought of Louise's father, whom she loved very much, but who was awful and mean to her, and basically just another phantom. She burst out aloud, "Maybe what everybody in the village tells me is true—I was hanging my hat too high. I should have known that he would never really stick around, and his family—they would never have wanted that for him." She thought of poor Louise, a very sensitive child. *If only he would at least acknowledge and communicate with Louise that would have made her feel better.* Louise's lack of love from a male figure that she could call a father tore at Naomi's inner soul. "*I hope she would not make the same mistake as me,*" Naomi said. Naomi was comforted by the fact that the majority of Barbadian black women were in a similar position, with their mothers fathering their children. "That is not right," she said angrily. "It just isn't right."

Naomi took her mind from this impediment, retracted, and continued to entertain exciting thoughts about leaving the sugar cane fields and working as a hawker selling sweets, at least for a start.

Of note is the fact that the production of sweets has been a cottage industry in Barbados for centuries. In early days, various kinds of candied fruits were shipped to England or sold to merchant ships calling at the island. Items included guava cheese, tamarind balls, shaddock rind, and sugar cakes.[1]

Naomi's imagination started to get the better of her. She envisaged moving on from just selling sweets to the preparation and selling of pudding and souse, another Bajan tradition on Saturdays. The main feature of this dish was the coiled intestines of pigs, which had to be thoroughly cleaned with soap and water in the process, turned inside out, and then soaked in salt water and lime juice for at least an hour. Sweet potato was then grated and mixed with ingredients such as thyme, red peppers, butter, some sugar, and some powdered clove. In days gone by, the pig's blood was used in the mixture with water added to give it its dark color. This mixture was then stuffed into the clean intestine, which was tied at both ends to prevent the mixture from escaping, after which, it was steamed or cooked slowly in boiling water until the mixture was cooked and the pig's intestine, or skins as it was called, was firm. The souse was made by dividing a pig's head in half. Washed, scraped, and cleaned well with a sharp knife, removing the brain in the process. It was then boiled in salted water until the flesh began to separate from the bones. The meat was then cut into pieces and placed in a bowl of pickles made from salt water, lime juice, chopped onion, cucumbers, and some red peppers added to make it spicier. It was left for many hours to steep before using. It was usually garnished with parsley.[2]

Naomi also considered making and selling another Barbadian traditional dish like conkies on Guy Fawkes Day, which was celebrated at that time.

In early November at least for a start, and depending on the response," she said "I will probably look at making the pudding and souse every Saturday. With all these thoughts racing through her head, Naomi suddenly felt reenergized.

---

[1]   *Author – Karl Watson, BARBADOS FIRST, The Years of Change, 1920 to 1970 (Page 93)*

[2]   *Author – Rita G. Springer, Caribbean Cookbook (Page 171)*

The origin of conkies is unknown, but it is said that it could be a corruption of the West African word kenky. Today, it is customary in Barbados to get conkies almost every day. One only has to find out who is selling them. They are, of course, available at some major supermarkets on the island.

Chapter 4

I T WAS THE year 1960. Louise, at eight, had been attending primary school since the age of five years, in uniform as was the custom, but barefoot of course. There was heat coming off the road, particularly on a very hot day, which incidentally was almost the norm. Louise tried not to let it bother her too much. Besides, most of the other children also went to school barefoot due to poverty like her. In most households, the wearing of shoes and socks to school was considered a luxury. Louise was a voracious reader, so in spite of her circumstances at home, which included using a torch light to read at night unknown to her mother, she continued to do so. Her mother would always tell her that the one kerosene oil lamp should not be used for reading as they had to stretch the kerosene because, in her own words, "Coppers [money] are scarce, so we have to economize." When Louise was unable to use the torchlight because the battery life hand ended, she read in the dark. Louise continued to perform well at the primary school that she attended. Her teacher Ms. Wilson was very pleased with her progress. Louise rarely required any discipline unlike other students who in some cases disrupted the class very frequently or did not do the homework assigned by the teacher at all.

Ms. Wilson would say to those guilty of this transgression, "You all would live to regret it one day." She also explained to her class that education was the only way out of poverty. Louise nodded her head in agreement with her teacher.

By the age of ten, Louise had developed so quickly that sometimes one or two classmates would make fun of her. Her breasts were budding very rapidly. Louise made a decision to pass certain games in the evening due to the rapid development. When she jumped, her budding breasts could be seen through her uniform. Louise was often embarrassed by this occurrence.

Louise's overall development continued at a rapid pace. During this time, Louise was allowed to sleep with her mother on their grass bed as there was no man in Naomi's life at this time 'passing through' while her siblings continued to sleep on the floor. One night, as Louise lay in bed, still at the tender age of ten, she felt something moist on her nightgown. Louise got up suddenly, touched her mom, with tears beginning to settle in her eyes, and she said, "Mother, get up. There is something damp on my nightgown." Naomi awakened, still drowsy after a long day's work as a laborer in the sugar cane fields, asked, "What is wrong with you, my dear child?" comforting her at the same time. Louise repeated, "There is something wet on my nightgown, and my molly [colloquial name for her vagina] feels damp." Naomi lit the kerosene oil lamp, which was kept nearby after removing the shade, then replaced it to get some light. Somehow, before she actually examined Louise, she just knew that the time had come for her to explain to Louise that her body was going through a change and what she should expect. Naomi always prayed that it would not come so soon as she considered Louise to be her baby, but she too marveled at Louise's rapid development and knew that her menstrual period was not the only thing she would have to talk to her about, that she would now have to gradually, but with a measure of urgency tell her about other things to protect her from boys and men in general and the implications of not doing so. Naomi however decided to put that off for as long as possible as to her it was still taboo.

Louise was also a very sociable child and tried to be everyone's friend. Still, there were some who because of Louise's light complexion and softer long hair, would say, *"Why she so poor-great though." (In Bajan dialect which is a unique language of Barbados poor-great means to act as if you are rich and a snob when in fact you are poor).*

By the time Louise reached the age of eleven, with her eleven-plus examination not far away, Louise was already wearing a bra. One evening just after school, Louise had this unfortunate incident that left her totally devastated! A group of girls headed by their ring leader, Margaret, who was a troublemaker, came over to her from behind. While grinning sarcastically she grabbed the middle section of Louise's uniform. Margaret then shouted to her cohorts, "See, I told you all so." Margaret continued, this time laughing out loudly, and said, "Louise's breasts are so huge she had to have them reined in by wearing a bra Ha-ha." Margaret laughed louder and louder. Other students joined in the loud laughter, surrounded Louise and started pulling and tugging at her inner blouse. They pulled so hard, that the blouse was totally torn apart, exposing her bra. They continued laughing and mocking her said, "She got big breasts, she got over flowing breasts." One student threw parts of her torn blouse in the air. Some began tugging at her bra, trying to tear it off too. Margaret, the main bully got hold of Louise's long hair which was plated in one, started pulling her by the hair. One student said, "You think because you have that light skin color and that 'good' hair, you better than us. And because teacher like you" Look! 'Tek dat' and spat in her face. *('Tek' is the Bajan for take and dat is the Bajan for that)* As if they had not done enough, the bully Margaret continued to pull her by her hair, dragging her a few yards away, which caused her to fall to the ground. Meanwhile other students continued chanting and clapping hands in sync, "She got big breasts, she got over flowing breast." Louise terrified and in tears tried to free her hair from Margaret's grip. When she finally succeeded, she got up and grabbed as much of her torn blouse from the ground as possible, ran as fast as she could, using the parts of her torn blouse, that she managed to salvage and tried to cover her breasts. However she stumbled and fell to the ground. Blood was dripping from her right knee which took the brunt of her injury. She was in pain, but struggled to hop along as fast as she could, to get away from these bullies.

Louise arrived home still crying and hyperventilating had difficulty speaking. Her mother very alarmed and livid said, "Lord Have Mercy. What happen? Why is your blouse all torn apart and why is your knee bleeding like that?" Louise, still hyperventilating, crying and stammering, said to her mother "the children in my class would not stop bullying me. I try so hard to be their friend, but they would not stop." Her mother said to her, "This can't end so. I am going to the Head Teacher 'bright' and early tomorrow morning and make an official complaint."

Louise started screaming, said "No mother! No! Please do not; if you complain to the Head Teacher, those horrible children will beat me up again." Her mother tried to calm her down said, "No Louise! You do not understand they would beat you up again if I do not make a formal complaint." Louise responded and said, mother! Please, listen to me! Maybe I should not have been born this color; I should be black like everyone else which leads me to ask you the same question that I have asked over and over again. Who is my father?" Naomi found herself between a rock and a hard place, ignored the question and said "My child come let me clean up the abrasion on your knee, place some plaster on it and then you go and get an early wash up. We will discuss this very bad situation tomorrow." Surprisingly Louise responded, "No we will not! Because if you do decide to make the complaint, I will NOT go back to that school" Naomi responded, "Are you crazy. The eleven –plus examination is a few weeks away, so you have to go back to school for revision." Louise sucked her teeth, and said, "Mother you hear what I tell you. I will NOT go back, even if you insist period." Actually Naomi had never seen her daughter so defiant. She gave Louise a very gently hug. She reminded her that she is beautiful and that most of the problem as she told her already was because of jealousy. She said, "It's not only the children in this village, it is also the grown-ups too, and even if your breasts were as flat as a pancake, they would still find something to be critical about you because they probably wish they had your color and hair, and looked like you, trust me."

That night as Louise knelt in pray beside the grass bed, she said, "Dear Lord, please do not let this happen to me again. Please make my breasts shrink. Thank you, dear Jesus. Amen." With that, she closed her eyes and tried to go to sleep by counting sheep. Her mother had told her some time ago that by so doing she would be able to erase any unpleasant occurrence and have a good night's rest. Louise quickly fell into a deep slumber. From that day onward at school, Louise introduced the defensive mechanism of raising both hands subconsciously in front of her chest in an effort to cover the presence of her growing breasts. (Unlike today, during that era in Barbados, early breast development in a girl was something that other girls generally looked down upon).

Chapter 5

A S THE MONTHS passed by Naomi became restless. Toiling and working very hard in the sugar cane fields cutting and loading canes day after day proved to be more difficult for her; and she began to question her long term endurance as a result. Meanwhile her friend Mildred was only working one day a week. Mildred's situation had improved dramatically, as her older son had migrated to the U.K. and was now sending funds to her on a steady basis.

It was a very hot day. Mildred was working that particular day. She, recognizing the bewildered look on Naomi's face said to her, "You do not look right, what is wrong?" Naomi sucked her teeth and said, "I am feeling extremely depressed." I really appreciate the help my first child Oswald is giving me with the cutting and loading of the canes. Lizzy and Avonda, my other two daughters, people in this village consider them to be dumb, but at least they are attending needle work classes with Ms. Bentham, who conducts the classes' three houses away from my house."

Naomi stopped briefly, wiped the sweat from her face with her apron said, "My beautiful last child Louise is doing extremely well at school, and I am very proud of her. However, my other two sons, they are bare stress. As you know they hardly went to school, and instead of finding gainful employment like how Oswald helps me out in the sugar cane fields, they refuse to do anything positive." Mildred responded and said, "That is not good at all." Naomi responded and said, "I don't know if I ever told you this before, but one is an alcoholic and the other is a gambler. All the talking and quarreling that I do have made no difference. At the rate they are going, I have to make sure that they don't send me in the mad house." Mildred replied, "What? At their age they are heavily involved in such negative behavior already. All I would advise you to do is to take it easy. Your life has been hard from day one. Don't let those two boys drive you crazy. Pray! Do what I tell you." Naomi responded, "Yes! I will take your advice."

Of all of her siblings, Louise always gravitated towards her big brother Oswald. He, like her brothers and sisters is of a dark/black complexion. One day while Oswald and Louise were on their make shift front step which was basically a huge stone, she looked at him intently and said, "You know you are my favorite brother." Oswald was very pleased to hear that. He said to her with excitement in his voice, "Oh yes! I am very proud of you 'sis. Your complexion is so light and flawless; you have such a pretty face and such 'nice hair, not nappy like Lizzy and Avonda's. It is for all of these reasons that I love you so very much. You make me very proud. You are the youngest and prettiest."

Louise became highly agitated said, "Rubbish! Stop it!" With a stern look on her face she said to him, "Enough of that nonsense. Why do you and others constantly say these things about me? I hate been told that all of the time. You are my brother so that even makes it worse. Besides, color and being pretty don't matter. All I want is to know my father. I constantly asking mother and she makes me angry, always changing the subject. I would prefer to be black like you all and at least know my father. Actually in case you do not realize it, I am sad most of the time, but I try really hard not to show it." He comforted her by placing his arms around her, and said," I am truly sorry that you don't know your father. Just try to cheer up a bit. That would make me very happy. Promise me." Louise shook her head and said to him, "I don't know if I can promise you that."

A week later while sitting on a bench outside of the village shop owned by Ms. Jones along with his friend John; playing a game of dominoes, Oswald continued to boast about his beautiful 'red' sister Louise. He said, "John! You see my little sister recently? Every day she is more beautiful than the day before. Nobody in this village can't get a sister looking like her. She has such a beautiful 'red' complexion and lovely hair, she is our star."

John became very agitated jumped up from the bench, slams down the dominoes which were in his hand, on the table, said to Oswald. "No offense to you, but I am sick and tired of hearing about your beautiful little sister Louise and her complexion all the time." John paused for a minute, looked as if in deep thought then continued and said, "But just a minute, who is 'she' father though? I hear about yours and the other brothers and sisters fathers, even though I know they did not 'stick' around, but I still can't figure out who is 'she' father, like she dropped down like manna from the sky!" John added with sarcastic laughter, "I hope for your sake that she has a long and happy life, Louise! Louise all the blasted time!"

To soften things up a bit, seeing the hurt and dejected look on Oswald's face, John patted him lightly on the back said, "Listen to me, we all know she is very pretty, but you don't have to constantly remind us. Look 'man', there are people in this village who have very low self-esteem because of their skin color, being black and their African features, and the fact that you constantly remind us of her beauty will only cause these people to feel more devalued, with little self-worth. Even your other two sisters, Lizzy and Avonda may be feeling that way too. The fact that they are fat and black, and you never say a kind word to them or about them, I am sure that it 'gets to them'." Oswald attempted to speak, but John got more agitated, pointed his finger at Oswald in an intimidating manner said, "Do you understand what I am saying? I meant to tell you a long time ago but now is just as good a time, because it is really getting out of hand. You behave as if your other sisters do not even exist, like you are ashamed of them."

John continued with more aggression, "You see this society here in Barbados; it is too full of this foolishness, defining someone based on their skin color. When are we going to break away from this Colonial nonsense? All of this talk about who red, who light skin and who black, it is a serious form of discrimination, one that has been going on for too long, and it has become endemic; and Oswald, you are making it worse within your family."

Oswald feebly puts up a defense said, "But John, you hit me real hard there with your harsh words. As for my other two sisters, the truth of the matter is they are fat and very lazy; all they do is eat non-stop, and seldom help my mother. When my mother and I come in on evenings from cutting and loading the canes, as big girls they should have our food ready, but No, mother has to come in and cook and you know what, all they do is just 'eat down' the whole house. And that is the truth. That is why I loathe them so very much."

John still with an angry look on his face and still in an agitated tone of voice and shouting louder said, "No offense to you again, but I am more educated than you are, and you might not fully understand where I am coming from, but by your own action in words and deeds towards both of them, those things might be contributing to their lazy lifestyle and eating habits. Maybe the girls feel hopeless with the constant comparison to their sister."

Oswald with a dejected look on his face said, "I understand where you are coming from but my own mother has repeatedly said to whoever would listen that nobody in this village can get a pretty light skinned child like her Louise." John sucked his teeth and said, "Your mother might also be saying that out of ignorance, just think about it, and the next time she goes down 'that road', tell 'she' politely that it does not matter who black, white, yellow or brown, all of 'we' are going the same place at some point in time. Let her know that she should love and embrace all of her children." To lighten things up John remarked "I finish with this conversation. But Oswald, you are still my best friend okay, no love lost."

Oswald shook his head in agreement. They then continued their game of dominoes, after which they both departed for home after giving each other a big friendly hug.

Chapter 6

THAT SAME DAY shortly after the outburst, Oswald arrived home. Meanwhile Lizzy and Avonda were outside sitting on the front step. Oswald beckoned to them to come inside and join him.

On entering, Lizzy burst out laughing, and in amazement said to Avonda sarcastically, "I wonder what this is all about? This is so unusual. Oswald actually wants to speak to us. The only good thing here is that he is not shouting at us for a change." Avonda responded and said, "Wow Oswald, what have we done wrong this time around?" He stared at both of them, then spontaneously, gave each sister a hug, after which he said, "Nothing my darling sisters, I just want to have a brotherly chat with you 'guys'. First of all to let you know how much I love you both."

Avonda jumped up and exclaimed! "What! You got to be kidding me. Hearing you say that is so strange. What has come over you all of a sudden, because the only person in this house apart from mother who matters to you is Louise." Then with one hand on her hip and with a slightly confrontational demeanor and harsh tone of voice, she continued, "Tell us please. Because you act all the time as if you are ashamed that we are your sisters, so what is new?" Oswald responded and said, "No! No! I sincerely love you both. Maybe I never showed my love for you all as I should have, and I am not making excuses, but I now know that it is because of how we here in Barbados have been socialized. My apologies to both of you."

Lizzy and Avonda now extremely surprise, gave Oswald a suspicious look. Then Lizzy interjected and said, "Yes, you never say a kind word to us or pay us a simple compliment. We always believe that we could never measure up to Louise in any way. You, like other people in this village think that we are fat, black and ugly, that is why we keep to ourselves. We love Louise dearly and she knows that. Ironically, yes. I do know that word even though I hardly went to school and everyone thinks that we are dumb, but we know that Louise never shares the same view as you all do." Avonda chimed in and said, "Yes that is true. Louise is such a sweet person. She will always be our darling little sister, but we are sick and tired of this color thing and who 'pretty'. A few days ago, when I introduced Louise to this person whom I felt should have known better, you want to know what she said to me. Wait! You are really 'she' sister, she so pretty, unlike you. Is she adopted? and laughed at me. I said to myself what the hell next?"

Lizzy interjected and said to Oswald, "You and others do not understand Louise. She even hates it when you and other people continue telling 'she' how pretty she is and what a beautiful light complexion she has."

Avonda added, "To be honest, I know Louise would prefer to be black like 'we', and know her father. She said so on numerous occasions, even if he did not support her than to not know him at all. It is people like you, in your case maybe unconsciously who think that the two of us are no more than failures." Tears settled in Oswald's eyes, he gestured with his hands in the air, and in an appealing tone said, "Stop there. No! No! Please listen to me for a moment. I must admit that I did fall into that category before whereby I always saw the complexion and the looks of a person and defined them accordingly, but I have now seen the light and I know that it is not the color or looks, it is the person." He paused for a moment. Then in a very definitive tone said to his sisters, "Going forward, please do not allow anyone to validate you all based on the color of your skin, looks or size. You are all beautiful and special to me and in the eyes of God, just as special as Louise. My thoughts were due to ignorance and how this Barbadian society as a whole categorize its people based on these superficial things. All I would like both of you all to do is concentrate on your sewing. It may look insignificant now, but I am sure it will help you all later in life. You all may even be able to go into fashion designing, you never know."

The two sisters looked relieved with big smiles on their faces, as if they felt liberated.

Avonda, now standing very erect said to Oswald, "On behalf of Lizzy and I, we thank you for your kind words. It is because of what you have just said that we no longer feel useless, ugly, fat, black, and down trodden. You will never know how much you have boosted our self-esteem. You have empowered us. And for us it is a new dawn and it is because of you that we now believe that the sky is the limit." Oswald with a radiant smile on his face gave each a big hug. Actually, it was as if he too felt liberated. He said to them, "You have both made me very happy. I must admit that my dear friend John played a huge role in allowing me to see the beauty within you all and people in general. There is too much emphasis on color and class in this island, which unfortunately defines all citizens, young and old alike."

Lizzy stood up and playfully touched Oswald's hair, said, "Ossie! See I am calling you by your 'nick' name now, so you can understand how much closer I now feel to you, because as you know, only Louise and mother call you Ossie. Anyway we thank you. We will now go outdoors and continue to spend the remainder of the evening in the open air to be with nature, and watch the sun set and the birds as they fly away to their nests."

Chapter 7

A S ALLUDED TO by Naomi, her other two sons, Peter and Fred were extremely problematic. Actually, Peter was classified as the rogue in the family. He started consuming alcohol at an early age. After finishing his food in the evening, he would go on the block 'liming' with the block boys. However, by night time, Peter would find himself in the village shop amongst all the older men who were 'hard line' drinkers. His favorite liquor was pure white rum.

It was late evening. Peter as usual went up the street, a few yards from the village shop, of course with a bottle of white rum in hand and sipping the rum constantly.

He bragged to one of his rum-drinking friends Andrew and said, "Once I got my rum, I real good." Andrew, while laughing gave Peter a 'high five' said, "I know 'man', nothing wrong with that."

As the sun went down, Peter hurried to the village shop. The owner Ms. Jones, who was behind the counter said to him, "Peter what you plan to do with your life? Your mother and older brother out there during crop season working hard in the blistering sun and you liming on the block during the day and a 'rummie' at night. You are not going to live too long if you go on at that rate."

Peter still with bottle of white rum in his hand, most of which he had already consumed, staggered from drinking all evening, pointed his finger at Ms. Jones with contempt and his crazy drunken eyes said to her, "Why you don't leave me alone? What my drinking has to do with you? For a big woman you too malicious. Why you don't mind your own business? Not even my mother that bring me into this fucking world can tell me what to do, far less you."

Ms. Jones in anger, shouted at him, while gesturing with her hand in the air said, "Oh yes! Why I don't mind my own business? Boy at the rate you going, you soon going to have a lot of your own business to mine. You don't know that even though I am selling it too much alcohol is bad for your heart, kidneys and all of your vital organs; and on top of it all, when you drink all of that rum; you get in my shop and swear like a pirate. Where is the respect boy? I am soon going to band you from coming in here."

Before anyone could say 'Jack Robin', Peter started swaying from side to side in a drunken state while saying, "Oh God, I am not feeling good. Somebody help me."

Peter wobbled over and leaned on the counter top for support. Next thing you know, Peter's vomit was coming up like a pipe that burst, all inside of Ms. Jones' shop, contaminating lots of the nearby items on sale.

Ms. Jones became livid, and said, "Look! You see what you just do." She got up from behind the counter and gave Peter one slap around his head and said, "Carry your ass from inside of my shop do. And hurry too."

Ms. Jones then beckoned to another 'rummie' name Philip while at the same time checking Philip's level of alertness said to him, while pointing, "Go down the road there at that small house to his mother Naomi, tell 'she' to come here right now, that her 'rummie' son just puke up the whole place. And tell 'she', she has to reimburse me too, so walk with 'she purse and also a mop bucket."

Ms. Jones followed Peter to the door, while saying, "You stupid ass bitch, don't come back in here, because if you come back in here, I am going to call the police and have you arrested. This is not the first time that you have made a mess of my stock and now I have to get all of that 'crap' clean up, thanks to ignorant ass you."

Peter was now higher than a kite, barely made it through the door, still wobbling and mumbling, "Oh Lord, somebody! Help me! I feel too sick though."

He attempted to cross the road, right in front of the shop, without looking left or right. Next thing you know, a truck came down at the same time full speed. There was a loud sound of screeching brakes. The driver, angry and mortified at what could have happened said to Peter, "Look 'carry' your ass out of the road."

Naomi, tired from a long day in the sugar cane fields arrived at the shop shortly after. She was very angry and agitated seeing the mess that Peter had made of several items in Ms. Jones' shop. She could not believe her eyes. She said, "Lord Look 'ma' crosses, ('ma' is Barbadian dialect for the word my) 'he' father that he 'don't know much about was an alcoholic, and it killed 'he', like the same thing going to happen to 'he' too. Oh Lord, I really need an intervention for 'he' before it is too late."

After cleaning the area, and looking very tired and bewildered, Naomi was very apologetic to Ms. Jones. She also said to her, "Look! Band 'he' from coming into your shop because this is bare stress. All Peter 'do' is carry away the little bit of money that I work so hard for in the sweltering heat, to get rum." Ms. Jones said to Naomi, "I don't know how you manage with that jack ass, a young boy like him, and that is the best he can do! I am very glad that you come so quickly, because I really can't take the stench of that puke." When Naomi enquired about the amount of money she had to pay for the spoiled items, Ms. Jones said to her, "You are such a wonderful woman, but I really don't envy you. Just give me what you can afford, but make sure that he does not set foot in my shop ever again." Naomi said, "I will see to that, and thank you for your gratitude."

Chapter 8

FRED, THE YOUNGER of the two out of control brothers would gamble all day and all night if he could. He would also steal his mother's money when he got desperate.

Early one morning, Naomi was ready for work, but was delayed as a result of not been able to find some money that she was trying to save to enable her to do some repairs to the house. She looked in every conceivable place, and was puzzled that she came up empty handed. She then confronted Fred, being aware that money had gone missing prior, and that he was the culprit.

She said to him, "Look! All you doing is carrying away my money. If you do not stop stealing the little bit I have to work so hard for, I am going to call the police for you. Both you and Peter are too disgusting and ungrateful. You gambling nonstop and he always drunk all over the place. How you all get so though?"

Fred with a smirk on his face said, "Well, maybe if we had a father or rather fathers in our lives to keep us in line, we would have turned out better, no disrespect to you though, but you mean you never thought about that."

Naomi was livid. She picked up the broom stick from a corner, and with it in the air swings it at Fred while saying, "Look you! Hold your 'horses', I don't want a lot of long talk from you, because you too disrespectful. I don't get any problem from Oswald, or the girls and I don't plan on putting up with you and your brother's nonsense all my life. I tell you already, I am going to call the police next time and let you end up in jail, because it is only then that you will get the message."

Fred still with a smirk on his face shifted his body to avoid any contact with the broom stick.

However Fred did not end up in jail, but due to an altercation ended up with a big gash on his head, which landed him in the hospital.

It was the following day. Naomi had just arrived home from work. She heard a loud persistent knock on the front door of their chattel house. While peeping through the flaps (window), she enquired who was there. At the same time, she recognized that it was one of Fred's friends whom he gambled with. In an impatient tone of voice, Jimmy said, "Ms. Naomi you better come up by the shop quick! Quick! Because Fred and one of the fellows who gambles with 'he', just had an altercation over money, and Fred up there bleeding from 'he' head very badly. The boy's name is Richard."

Naomi rushed up the street. A few yards from Ms. Jones' shop, she saw Fred lying on the ground with a big 'gash' to his head bleeding profusely. She, extremely alarmed, touched her forehead while saying, "Oh Lord! Help my son; don't let 'he' die."

She then held her belly in anguish at the sight of the blood pouring down on the pavement. She screamed out in agony said, "Lord my belly! my belly! Somebody call the ambulance quick."

One of the guys who gambled too, but who was not involved in the altercation ran into Ms. Jones' shop and asked to use the phone. He called the hospital, and requested that an ambulance be sent right away. Meanwhile, Naomi ran over to where her son was lying.

Richard was over him placing pressure on the wound to stop the flow of blood with a piece of cloth. She snatched the white cloth from Richard's hand and started to apply pressure on the wound to stop the bleeding herself and said, "Look! Give me that, and get out of my way fast too, before I 'lick' you down."

Richard, with a scared and alarmed look on his face, said to her, "Mistress, my apologies to you. Hear what happen. I won the game but Fred cheated me, and he always cheating and taking advantage of me and he carried away all of my money too. So I get real angry and I 'snap'. He and I had a fight and I hit 'he' on 'he' head with a glass bottle, so he got the worse of it. But I real sorry though. Besides Fred is my friend, so please don't call the police for me. I beg you!"

Naomi stared at Richard while she shook her head from side to side. She then allowed Richard to continue to apply the pressure on the wound until the ambulance arrived. On its arrival, Naomi accompanied Fred to the hospital. The doctor who examined the 'wound', cleaned the area, applied appropriate solution, and then bandaged Fred's head. He told her that Fred was lucky, that if the chop had gone further down, it would have been life threatening.

One morning, a few months later, before Naomi left for work Fred told his mother that he would like to have a chat with her, preferably right away; and that Peter would be present. Naomi responded, "Chat! Don't tell me you all in trouble again. You all like you want to see me six feet under." Fred said, "Please mother." Naomi was taken by surprise to see this non-confrontational behavior, knowing that both Fred and Peter had no respect for her whatsoever.

Peter quickly appeared. She finally agreed to hear them out. Fred informed her that Oswald arranged to have his friend John speak to both of them about their total disrespect, bad attitude, and most of all their addiction to alcohol and gambling; and that coming out of the meeting, John had emphasized their need to be respectful to her, show love and appreciation and also the fact that she had toiled all her life on her own to make 'ends meet' for all of them, that she deserved better.

Peter interjected and said that part of the meet dealt with their vices, and admitted that they wanted to give up their 'demons, acknowledging that being so young with these vices were very bad for them, and could only get worse over time'. That the good news is that John was able to speak with individuals who would gradually help them through their addictions. Peter apologized to her for their indifference and disrespect towards her. They both agreed to help her out in the sugar cane fields, while also seeking out a trade that both of them, if successful, would eventually be able to contribute towards the household in a more meaningful way. Naomi was shocked, but overjoyed. She gave each of them a hug and told them that they had made her day.

They both also acknowledged that they could have been dead as a result of the path they had taken, and that it was a second chance for them to truly make a difference.

Chapter 9

THE TIME FOR the eleven-plus examination was quickly approaching. Ms. Wilson, Louise's teacher spent hours during lunch break and after school giving her students lessons. Ms. Wilson took pride in her job as a teacher. She felt that, given the extra push, her students could do well, even though the majority was still poor and downtrodden. Ms. Wilson reminded herself, but who in this village is not poor? I can count only two families. Both of these families ran a village shop. Evidence of this stratum of the society was clear. In one case, members of one family, a son and daughter, were able to wear shoes and socks and, in the case of the daughter, ribbons to school each day. The other family was able to send their two daughters to school not only decked out in shoes and socks and ribbons, but they were chauffeur driven in the family's black car. Those children were treated like royalty by both students and teachers. It must be noted that ownership of cars in those days was a privilege designated to only a few, and the main color of the cars was black.

The day of the eleven-plus examination to see who would get into the so-called 'good' schools on the island came and passed and was considered uneventful apart from the anxious parents who waited with bated breath to hear all about how well their sons/daughters/wards had done.

Of note, the eleven-plus examination in Barbados is like a rite of passage. All things being equal, each child in Barbados is expected to take this exam. There have been several arguments for and against this examination. Some argue that it is the fairest system. Yet some say that it creates a type of stigma that follows those that are considered underachievers and who passed for the so-called newer secondary schools and that they are never able to throw it from their past irrespective of the heights some of them may reach as adults in their chosen careers.

Today, there are twenty-two secondary schools in Barbados, with a minimum number of privately owned secondary schools. However, many of the newer secondary schools did not exist during Louise's time at school.

There is also presently free education in Barbados from nursery to university level for all its citizens. The campus at Cave Hill, Saint Michael, is a branch of the University of the West Indies. The other two campuses are located in Trinidad and Jamaica respectively. The University of the West Indies is very well recognized worldwide, and the subject content in the respective faculty is comparable to other universities in more developed countries. Free education until university level is quite a feat for a small developing nation like Barbados with no natural resources. Access to free education has propelled many families from the poverty that transcended almost every family when Louise attended primary school. Today, in spite of the free education for all and the highly competitive atmosphere in terms of aspirations and goals, there are a percentage of children who still fall through the cracks mainly due to their socioeconomic situation. In some cases, households at the bottom of the hierarchy are unable or unwilling to break the cycle whereby the girl children become young mothers, and their girl children in turn, upon attaining the age of puberty also become young mothers.

The days were going by quickly. It was now the end of May almost time for the results of the eleven-plus examination to be announced. As the countdown continued, teachers, parents, and students anxiously awaited that announcement.

Finally, the day came. During the afternoon session, Ms. Wilson informed her students of the important announcement she had to make and said that she would do so shortly. An eerie calmness engulfed the classroom. All her students waited in anticipation.

That evening, Louise ran as fast as her legs would carry her from school to home. She said, "Mother, Mother, I made it, I made it."

"What?" Naomi asked. She hadn't seen Louise so happy in a long time. Louise responded, "I made it for a 'good' school." Naomi was barely able to contain her excitement too. She said, "I told you so. You are not only pretty, you are smart."

Louise said, "Oh, Mother, please, not again! Stop telling me I am pretty. Why does everyone say that anyway?" Naomi responded, "Because you are." Louise looked at her mother with a distant expression on her face and said, "Mother, I am very happy and excited to attend my new school. But I am sad because everyone tells me I am pretty and that I am the splitting image of my father, but Mother where is my father? I do not even know my father, and my patience is running out in case you do not realize it."

Naomi, as happened in the past looked at her daughter in despair and said, "Let's talk about him another time."

Chapter 10

IT WAS A week before Christmas. Louise was now twelve going thirteen. She was settled in her new school and was very attentive not only in the classroom but with regard to doing homework that was assigned to her by her respective teachers. Louise tried to find excuses for not participating in physical exercises that would cause her body to move around too much. She insisted to herself that her boobs were a hindrance because of their size, constantly growing and juggling at every opportunity. However, the taunts that followed her at primary school with regard to the size of her breasts were now a thing of the past. For that she was thankful.

It was Friday evening, Naomi and Mildred had just finished work in the sugar cane fields. Naomi with excitement in her voice said to Mildred, "I wanted to share some good news with you all day." Mildred said, tell me quickly. Naomi said, "I met this new man recently. I have fallen hard for him, and based on our conversations I feel he is different from all the other men who came into my life for a free ride; and that he would help me out with my children, as he seems very interested in their welfare, and you know for me right now that is a priority, His name is Geoffrey." Mildred responded,

"Wow! Sounds good, and with six mouths to feed, you really need a good steady man, so I am very happy for you."

It is 5:00 p.m. same evening, Naomi arrived home. She bathes quickly in the yard, and then dresses in a pants and top. She proceeds to make her face more attractive. She firstly looked through the window, and called out to Louise who was outside sitting on the front step. She said, "Louise! Come here, I need some help from you with my hair." Naomi looking into the mirror powders her face and applied some lipstick. Louise quickly appeared. She said to her mother, "Wow! Your hair is not yet done but you look very nice already." Naomi said, "Thanks, but I need some help with my hair." Louise pinned up her mother's hair. After examining her mother's face, Louise removed some of the lipstick that was not quite on her mother's lips, she then used the same lipstick and applied a bit on her mother's cheeks, blended with powder to appear like blush. Louise stepped back when done and said to her mother, "You look extremely lovely, where are you going? Do you have a date?"

Naomi responded and said "My dear, I am going nowhere. But the date is coming here." With excitement Naomi said to Louise, "Go call the others. Tell them to hurry and come quickly!" Louise went outside, saw her siblings a good distance away kicking ball with two of the neighbors. She shouted loudly to them, while gesturing with her hand said, "Hey You all, Come! Come! Mother wants you to come inside right away. Please hurry."

They all came at full speed racing in her direction to see which of them would get inside first. On arrival home they were all out of breath, they bundled together, apart from Oswald who was slightly ahead. As soon as they entered, Oswald recognized the transformation in his mother's face and attire said, "Wow! You look so stunning, this better be important, because I am out of breath from rushing and need some water."

Oswald gulped down the water from an enamel cup which was taken from a bucket on the kitchen table. The others took turn drinking water also. Every one of them sat at the table on the two benches in the 'shed roof' (Shed roof, equivalent to a dining room, but much smaller.)

It is a few minutes to 6:00 p.m. Naomi beamed with excitement, rapidly rubbed the palms of her hands and announced to her children, "I am very pleased to let you all know that there is a new man in my life. His name is Geoffrey and he will be here soon." Oswald grinned, and said; "Now I know why you are all dressed up. We are very happy for you." The other siblings clapped hands spontaneously, and then gave each other a high five in tandem. Oswald said, "Well! Well! Imagine mother madly in love like a school girl." She shrugged her shoulders while pretending to walk with flair with a huge smile on her face. She then said, "From what I see, and observe he is the best man I ever had. Not like you all worthless fathers. You all in realize that I kick Beresford to the curb too." Oswald quickly said, "I did"

At 6.30 p.m. there was a loud knock on the front door. Naomi rushed to open. Geoffrey entered with a broad smile on his face. He bend over, kissed Naomi on her cheek. He then said, "Good Evening. Nice family." With pure unbridled joy on her face, Naomi gazed into his eyes, and proceeded to introduce her children one by one. Geoffrey's hand shake of the first five was motionless, but when he got to Louise, he gazed at her intently with an initial surprise look on his face; suddenly he greeted her with a huge hug and smile. Geoffrey at that point, declared to Naomi, "I intend to be part of your wonderful family." On hearing that statement Naomi still beaming with excitement said, "I know you will," While giving him another kiss on the cheek.

On Christmas Eve, there were the usual traditions where the children were able to acquire marl and spread it around the yard after cleaning every part of their modest house. They were also able to make a Christmas tree from branches they had plucked from the Mile tree. For decorations, Geoffrey gave the children a few dollars and told them that they should get some foil paper with the money and anything else they saw at the shop that they could use on the tree. That they did. In addition to covering some of the branches with the foil, they also made balls from the foil. There were no gifts to be had in this household to place under the tree. There was nothing unusual about that. However, the children improvised by covering two shoeboxes that were given to them by a neighbor with foil paper and they utilized some red and green strips of cloth around the boxes.

Everyone also assisted with the newly stitched curtains, putting them up at the few windows in their small chattel house. Geoffrey even offered to paint small parts of the interior of the wooden house—the parts that were good and not worm eaten. According to Geoffrey, "This would make the house feel more like Christmas." As an afterthought, Geoffrey gave each child a two-dollar bill as his gift to them for Christmas. All in all, they were satisfied. He reminded them that the two dollars for the gift excluded the money that he had given their mother to purchase their church attire.

However, unknown to the other siblings, Geoffrey gave Louise a ten-dollar bill. He told her that he thought she was very pretty and that he did not only mean her face—that she was pretty all over from her head to toes. He said, "Louise! That is between you and me. That is our secret. I am going to take good care of you. You must not ever mention any of what I have told you to your mother because she might see it differently from the way it is, and I don't want any stress from her, okay? Promise!"

Louise nodded her head in the affirmative. Louise was very happy that there was now a father figure in her life. She, like all her siblings, called him Uncle. Louise said to Geoffrey, "Uncle, this is going to be my best Christmas ever because now I have you in my life. I now have a dad."

Geoffrey had a broad smile on his face. He responded and said, "Yes, my angel, that is so true." Geoffrey was not oblivious to Louise's growing maturity. Geoffrey got up from where he was sitting, which was only a few yards away from Louise. He took one hard, longing look at Louise's almost-voluptuous body—the prominent breast, her well-rounded butt, glowing skin tone, and beautiful long black hair. Geoffrey said to himself, *this is truly going to be some man's prized possession, wow! Sooner rather than later, but I have to figure out the right way to get it.*

Geoffrey became so consumed with his thoughts that before he knew it, the excitement that resulted got the better of him.

He looked downward, smoothened out his pants and then quickly got up from sitting, and gave Louise a quick peck on her cheek while saying, "See you tomorrow, my beautiful angel." Louise responded by returning a kiss on his cheek while saying, "Bye, Uncle." Geoffrey momentarily forgot what he was about to say before departure, and then said to Louise, "Louise, did your mother allow you to get the dress you wanted for church that I told you all about? I gave her the money and told her to make sure all of you get something nice for Christmas morning in the park, especially you, Louise." Louise became very excited, saying, "Thank you again, Uncle. That was so sweet of you," while reminding him that because of his actions, it would be "my best Christmas ever." She referred to the outfit again and said, "You're buying me my Christmas dress means so much to me." She laughingly said, "You are my uncle-daddy." Geoffrey said, "Oh, Louise that is nothing. There is so much more I have to give you. You are very special to me, always remember that." Louise responded, "I will, and thank you so much again."

It was now approaching bedtime. Naomi said to the children, "It is time to go to bed, children. Remember, you all have to get up early to go to church then to Queen's Park tomorrow morning, Christmas morning." She laid the girls' dresses on the grass bed and also the boys' shirts and pants. Naomi said, "Look, everything is here for tomorrow morning. The shoes and socks too. I will go get some rest now for an hour and get up by eleven p.m. and bake the coconut bread and pudding. I shan't bother to go to midnight mass because for the first time in a long time, we will all go to Queen's Park after church as a family, and besides I still have lots to do."

Going to the Queen's Park on Christmas morning is a Barbadian tradition which many Barbadians and visitors alike look forward to with anticipation; most are usually decked out in their finery.

A traditional ham was out of the question but the children were satisfied to know that their mother had already killed a fowl and it was now in lime and salt, waiting to be cooked early on Christmas morning after it was fully seasoned. Besides, with Geoffrey now in the picture, Naomi said she was feeling less stressed. She marveled at the fact that this was the first time since being a mother that she really was looking forward to the Christmas traditions in a big way.

Naomi's brain started to work in overdrive. She said to herself, "Once Geoffrey sticks around and continues to assist my New Year will be brighter than any other I have ever had. I might even be able to get out of the sugar cane fields sooner than I imagined and start selling my sweets—toffees, comforts, paradise plums, nut cake, and sugar cakes— and gradually add my pudding and souse and conkies to my sales." Naomi thought of the initial money she would need to aid her in getting started.

She again said to herself, "*Lord, I thank you for bringing Geoffrey into our lives.*" Besides, it didn't take much to make her happy. Naomi had been at such a low point economically like many of the other struggling single mothers in Barbados all her life that even the thoughts of a fraction of a better life gave her much joy and satisfaction as it was something to look forward to.

Chapter 11

T HE NEW YEAR came, and to Naomi, everything was falling into place. Geoffrey promised that he would help her with the new venture, and he said, "I am going to get you out of the sugar cane fields, Naomi, you deserve better. You are a good person. I will stick with you and the family through thick and thin." There was pure, unbridled joy on Naomi's face. She expressed her gratitude to Geoffrey. Naomi said to herself, *As Louise's always wish for we now have a father figure in our house.* She was happy for Louise in particular because unlike her other siblings, Louise continued to yearn for a father figure; and to Naomi, everything was now falling into place. "One big happy family with Geoffrey's constant presence," she said softly to herself.

Geoffrey was now spending every night there, unlike Naomi's previous partners, who would come one night and sleep and then several weeks in most cases would pass before she laid eyes on them. Then her fears would become a reality; it always happened. Eventually, they would just drift away permanently. It would be as if they were never there. No communication, nothing.

Naomi wondered if she was the problem, but she quickly erased those thoughts from her head as all the women she knew in the village basically told the same story.

Louise's passion for her school and all it had to offer continued. She excelled at most subjects, her favorites being English and Mathematics. Her deportment was excellent. She had joined the debating club and the school's newspaper, where she was elected sub editor. The girls Lizzy and Avonda continued with their needle work classes, at Ms. Bentham's house in the village. Ms. Bentham was one of those dressmakers who tried to facilitate everyone, even when they could not afford to pay her for the clothes she made for them, which was quite often. The girls got a stipend like other girls in the village who attended the needlework classes. Peter and Fred no longer 'hanged' out on the block, they showed greater appreciation to their mother and had now thankfully given up their demons, after counseling. They also pledged as often as possible to help out their mother in the sugar cane fields; in addition to trying their hands at carpentry from time to time once there was work available in the village. Everyone in the household appeared quite contented.

However, something strange was happening in Naomi's household. Naomi appreciated the help she got from Geoffrey, but when it came to their personal relationship, she sensed a change. She wondered if Geoffrey was now taking a fancy to someone else in the village, which was her history with all the men in her life. Naomi remained focused and upbeat in spite of these suspicions. She however, was getting a bit irritated at times as she felt that it was about time that Geoffrey really helped her out with the extra money he promised her to get her out of the sugar cane fields and start her goal of selling the sweets and with luck the additional items like the pudding and souse on Saturdays and, hopefully, the conkies.

Geoffrey, unknown to Naomi, started to come to her house around three in the afternoon or shortly thereafter which was the time Louise usually arrived home from school. For some reason, Geoffrey would surprise Louise with a lollipop after giving her an extra two dollars every evening as pocket money for the next day.

Louise would innocently say, "Uncle thanks but I am thirteen now. I don't need a lollipop every evening. I like them, but you don't have to do so every evening." Geoffrey would always say, "Louise, it is okay. You are special to me. You must remember that."

Geoffrey had no interest in Louise's older sisters. As far as he was concerned, they were both too black, with 'picky' hair. He would sometimes mutter under his breath, "And they are both ugly too." Not that Geoffrey was handsome; as a matter of fact, it was like the pot calling the kettle black. Truthfully, their resemblance to him was so striking he could have passed for their father, especially that of Lizzy, the older of the two sisters.

Chapter 12

I T WAS ALMOST summer vacation. Louise was happy to be going on vacation. She knew she had to find something meaningful to do all summer. She thought of the sports club that was recently formed in the village. She considered net ball, as she was informed that it would be one of the main sporting activities for the girls at the sports club. *"No,"* She said to herself, still very conscious of how rapidly her breasts continued to develop. *"Such an activity would certainly draw attention to them."* For her, that was a definite no-no. Louise said to herself upon heading out of the classroom as the school bell rang to signify the end of classes for the day, *"Maybe Uncle would be able to suggest some activity. I will ask him later tonight once I see him."*

On arrival home from school, she was pleasantly surprised to see Geoffrey already in the shed roof as if in deep thought. "Good evening, Uncle," she said.

"Good evening, Louise," Geoffrey said. "Come and give your Uncle a kiss."

Louise went over and gave him a peck on the cheek. Geoffrey held on to her for a few seconds, and then laughingly said, "Oh that feels so good!" Then with a charming smile on his face, he said, "You know, I am not going to wash my face tonight. I can't afford to wash your kiss off." Louise just giggled and said, "You are so funny, Uncle, that is what I like about you."

Louise quickly undressed and changed into a shorts and a top. Geoffrey said, "That was quick, Louise." Louise responded, "Yes, Uncle you are so right." She then remarked to him, "Uncle, this is the last week of school. I don't want to be bored stiff. Any suggestions as to how I can spend the summer vacation?" Geoffrey looked up at the galvanized roof. "Let's see." Then he said to her, "How about playing card games? I can teach you, and I can also buy you a snakes and ladders game, and you and I can play both cards and snakes and ladders. How about that?" Louise responded, "Uncle that sounds great. I knew you would be able to solve the problem of my potential boredom. Now I will have something to look forward to."

Geoffrey remained at Naomi's house until well into the night. Most of that time, his focus was on Louise. He sat at the table where she was sitting. He wanted to know all about her schoolwork—how she was coping with Spanish, which was the foreign language she chose over French. Did she like geography? And he went on and on. By 10:00 p.m., Louise said to him, "I am getting sleepy, Uncle. Tomorrow is still school. Vacation starts at the end of next week." Geoffrey was very apologetic and said, "Oh yes that is true."

The other siblings were already on the wooden floor fast asleep. Naomi had already retired to the grass bed after a very hard day's work in the sugar cane fields. Geoffrey said to Louise, who slept with her mother as long as Geoffrey was not going to be sleeping over, "Louise, I will wait until you change into your nightgown, then I will leave." Louise was so immersed all night talking with Geoffrey she forgot to wash up. Apart from a pit toilet in the yard, there was no bathroom facility in the house. There was now thankfully, a pipe in the yard. Geoffrey was instrumental in helping with this pipe.

Previously, the children had to draw water from the standpipe, which was a public pipe where most villagers drew their water from.

With this new luxury everyone in the household took their baths under this pipe in the morning, but in the evenings they would all wash up or by definition, they referred to it as washing their face and hands. This washing up was done by pouring water from the pipe into a basin in the tiny makeshift kitchen area.

Geoffrey offered to get the water from the pipe in the basin for Louise to wash up. This washing up centered on the washing of the face, hands, and privates. He said, "Louise, I will wait until you are finished to make sure you are okay."

"Thanks, Uncle," Louise said. Geoffrey went into the shed roof while Louise proceeded with her wash up. Louise washed up with total abandon, unaware that Geoffrey was gazing at her through the partially opened makeshift door that led from the shed roof to the kitchen.

Geoffrey was so elated with what he had just witnessed that he almost could not contain his excitement. As Louise came through the partially opened doorway, now with the towel in hand, and a change from clothing to night gown. Geoffrey said to Louise, "Come and give Uncle a kiss." Louise bent over and kissed him on the cheek. Geoffrey said, "This is really a bonus. It is the second kiss for the evening I managed to get from you." He added, "I am going to have some really sweet dreams tonight thanks to you." Louise then innocently wished him a good night. Geoffrey left momentarily but not before giving her another hard and longing look.

It was the last day of school before the summer holiday began. Louise was quite pleased with her performance in all her subjects. Apart from physical education in which she scored a grade F, her grades were excellent. She wanted to make her mother proud. As for what she wanted to do after the completion of school, she had not given that much thought.

The only place that she knew she would not be going was in the sugar cane fields like her mother. Louise was happy that times had really changed. Her mother also told her that during her time as a young girl there was hardly any opportunity for upward mobility; but with the additional secondary schools in Barbados now which were referred to as the newer secondary schools there was hope for many. She felt proud that she had passed the eleven-plus for one of the older secondary schools. As a matter of fact Louise was the only one of Naomi's children that made the grade for an older secondary school.

Chapter 13

I T WAS MONDAY evening, the first day of the vacation. The majority of the day was rather quiet for Louise. She hardly ventured out to play with the children in the village due to her "constraints" she would always remind herself. Many of the other children in the village heckled her anyway; they repeatedly referred to her as poor-great. And just because she had light skin or, rather, red as they often referred to her as, and the fact that she had long hair, they too believed she thought that she was better than they were. Louise hated that portrayal of her. She, however, remained resolute and determined and would always remind herself, "I am who I am and I will continue to keep my head up high like Mother suggested to me." One neighbor even referred to Louise as a haughty pig. That was so not the case. Louise was respectful to everyone. Besides, her mother would also remind her, "Girl, that pretty light skin color you have there is a bother to all of these people. They are all jealous of you, young and old. I am too glad for you. I am ugly and black and my nose is as flat as a pancake, but you really take after your father. I know one day, you going to make me proud."

On hearing the word *father*, Louise again asked, "But Mother, don't you have any photos of him? I have asked you so many times about him, yet no answer." With a sad look on her face her mother said, "My child, I prefer not to talk about him, I keep telling you so. Besides, you have Uncle Geoffrey anyway. He is the best man I ever was friends with. All the others are just a pack of no-good dogs." Louise, smiling, said, "Yes, Mother, Uncle is really good to me. I am glad that you have found him."

That statement brought joy to Naomi's face. She was not sad anymore for Louise—actually, she felt proud. That at least, was one achievement after questioning herself on many occasions, asking, "But why am I so unlucky with men? They have all used me and then leave me like a piece of trash." Memories of all her children's fathers again came back to haunt her. One by one, it happened over and over again. It was like a recurring decimal. Besides, it always happened after they bred her, she said to herself. Naomi had her first child at the age of fifteen from Mike, who also lived in the village, a few houses from her mother's shack. With no reliable form of contraceptives, by the age of twenty-six, she had six children— Louise being the last. The last and the prettiest. Naomi's thoughts started to wander again. What if Louise's father had been kind to her and stuck around? That would have been so nice. However, the class system, which lingered from the colonial past, would never have allowed that. Charles' family were too upper-class for her. As her mother said to her one day, (after discovering whom Naomi had 'lie down for', thus producing Louise) "Naomi, you hang your hat too high allowing the Overseer to breed you, that is the problem."

That second night of the summer vacation would be a turning point for Louise. Geoffrey came over around 8:00 p.m., giving everyone a warm good-night welcome and literally chatted away with Louise's siblings. That might have been construed as strange because apart from Louise Geoffrey rarely said much to her brothers and sisters. It was indeed an anomaly as Geoffrey's rationale for not saying too much was that as far as he was concerned, they were not his type. Of course, he could not tell this to Naomi. He said to himself that they were too rough, loud, and on top of it all, they were uneducated, having only completed primary school, and in the case of one of Louise's sisters and one brother, they did not even complete primary school. Louise was the gem in the household. That was Geoffrey's view. She had beauty and brilliance going for her. He said to himself, *"A man can't want it any better."*

It was approximately 9:00 p.m. when Geoffrey asked Louise if she wanted to play a card game with him and that he could teach her several others. The first game that Geoffrey agreed to teach her was go to pack as, in his view, it was easy to learn and quite relaxing. Before they both knew it, it was approaching 9:45 p.m. By then, everyone else had gone to sleep, including Louise's mother.

Geoffrey suddenly declared that Louise had learned the game quite quickly. He said to Louise, "We need to add some spice to this game to make it more exciting." Louise said excitedly, "And how do you propose to do that?" Geoffrey said, "Let's see—first, have you washed up yet?" Louise responded and said, "Not yet, Uncle." Geoffrey said, "Okay, it is getting late, and it would be better if you go wash up and get that out of the way. I will wait here for you." Geoffrey added, "Let me go and fill the basin with the water for you." Louise said, "Yes, Uncle, that would be nice. That way, when I am really sleepy I would have gotten that out of the way." Louise proceeded to the kitchen area with her nightgown in hand and a towel. Geoffrey ensured that the makeshift door to the kitchen was left slightly ajar again. Louise, innocently, went through with the exercise, unaware that her Uncle Geoffrey was taking in every moment of this essential activity. Frankly, it was a form of voyeurism for him. Geoffrey got so excited gazing at Louise's voluptuous breasts in clear view that he had some difficulty containing himself. He got even more excited when she proceeded to wash her privates. He said to himself, *here goes another windfall—oh, how I love it.*

After completion of the process, which included drying specific areas of her body very thoroughly, Louise exited the makeshift kitchen and proceeded to the shed roof where Geoffrey was sitting and waiting for her to join him. Geoffrey said, "Louise, are you sleepy yet?" Louise responded, "No, Uncle, I am not." Geoffrey said, "Well, my dear child,"— placing Louise's hand in his while gently massaging the palm—"these last set of games are going to be more competitive."

"What do you mean?" Louise asked. Geoffrey responded, "To make things more exciting, for each game you win, I will reward you monetarily." Louise said, "Oh, Uncle, really?" Geoffrey said, "Yes, my dear child, and if I win, let's see, I will give you some instructions, okay? Nothing to worry about, it's just a game. Is that cool with you?" Louise nodded her head in the affirmative while looking a bit bewildered.

At the onset of this last set of card games, Geoffrey allowed Louise to win the first four games. By now, Louise was doing pretty well with the game go to pack, or so she thought. Louise was elated as Geoffrey took ten dollars on each occasion, and said to her, "Look, you are taking all of my money, but never mind, we have an agreement, and you know what an agreement is, right?" Louise responded, "Yes, Uncle, I am not stupid. I just need to know, if I lose, what is your part of the agreement going to be?" Geoffrey said to Louise, "Okay, I will let you know momentarily, but you must keep your end of the bargain. Promise! Before I let you in on it." Geoffrey reiterated that she must keep her end of the bargain, and then added, "But of course, this is just between you and I, Okay? "Promise!" Louise, in her naïveté, said, "Yes, Uncle. I understand," but with an anxious look on her face. Geoffrey said, "You must not worry if I win the last game because I would never harm you in any way. Remember, it is just a game, and the agreement part is to make our games more exciting, okay!"

At the end of the fifth and last game, which intentionally but unknown to Louise, Geoffrey won, he said to her, "Now Louise, my dear child I have made you happy tonight. You have forty dollars to buy whatever you want to, and that as you know is a lot of money to be given in one night, right!" Louise said, "Yes Uncle." Geoffrey reminded Louise again, "I kept my end of the agreement and now I want you to keep your end too." Louise gazed at him still with some curiosity said, "But of course we have already both agreed. I just need to know what your part of the agreement will be because I have the forty dollars, and I cannot give it back to you because that would not be fun." Geoffrey reassured her that she would keep her money and repeated what he said earlier. Geoffrey also told Louise, "In addition to keeping the promise it is our 'special game,' and you mustn't tell anyone, no one—your brothers, sisters, mother, or anyone. We do not wish to have our games interrupted, so that's the other end of our bargain. You must be absolutely quiet about it, okay, and promise!" Louise nodded her head in the affirmative. At that point Geoffrey started to remove his belt from his waist while urging Louise to assist him. He said to her, "This is your part of the agreement; I won this game so now I get to tell you what to do." Louise looked a bit puzzled but said, "Okay."

Suddenly, like an act of divine intervention there was the sound of footsteps and Louise's mother appeared looking quite ruffled. She said, "Oh dear, I am having much difficulty sleeping. I have this terrible headache that would not go away," She continued, "I believe I caught a draught today while digging for yams in the field. The day was extremely hot and a heavy shower came down and I got soaked. I think I am getting really sick as a result."

Of course Geoffrey was upset by this sudden interruption to his plan but tried not to make it too obvious, he said to himself, *A man can't even get a little peace and quiet when he really needs it. Now this is really tough luck for me.* He was however grateful that Louise's mother had not detected any awkward moment, at least, he said to himself, it *does not appear to be the case.*

Reality stepped in, and he quickly asked Naomi, "Do you want me to get you some 'smelling salts'. I really do not like the way you look. You look more than sick and it would be unfair of me to continue the card game." He added, "I am sure Louise would understand, right Louise." Louise responded in the affirmative, and went over to where her mother was standing, and gave her a hug, while saying, "Mother, I hope that you will be alright." Naomi responded in a weak tone of voice saying, "Don't worry my child, I am sure I will be better soon."

And added, "Thank you both for your concerns, and Geoffrey I don't want to disrupt your game of cards with Louise—like you all are having lots of fun playing your game. Besides, once Louise is happy I am happy too." Naomi in her naiveté did not for one minute sensed that there was a remote possibility of anything 'going on', except a game of cards.

After Louise's mother went back to the grass bed, Geoffrey the 'low life' he was, declared "That was a huge interruption Louise," and as if his patience had ran out, immediately 'planted' a kiss on Louise's lips, while stroking her lovely black hair. This was a new development, as Geoffrey always kissed Louise on the cheek or forehead. Geoffrey then said to Louise, "Both of us are now happy, and we have both kept our end of the bargain." Louise gazed at Geoffrey, looking bewildered and shy with a faint half smile on her face, but this was not a real smile. In reality it was part of the tension and apprehension she was feeling that resonated in the form of a smile, said, "Yes, Uncle." Geoffrey reminded Louise again that this was their secret and asked her to make a pact that she would tell absolutely no one. "You know, Louise, if you even remotely utter one single word about this to anyone, I mean anyone—are you listening, Louise? That would be big-time trouble, not only for me but for you. This is our fun game, okay. Promise!" Louise nodded her head then softly said to him, "I promise, Uncle."

It was now just after 10:00 p.m. Geoffrey checked to ensure that the house was as secure as possible given the rundown condition, then kissed her on the cheek and wished her a very good night.

Chapter 14

L OUISE DID NOT see Geoffrey the following day. During the day, which was Tuesday, Louise went to the beach with her brother Oswald. The sun was brilliant, and the sea water was crystal clear. The waves were perfect too. Louise really had lots of fun frolicking in the water with Oswald throwing sand on her and she in turn throwing the sand back at him.

Oswald, out of the blue, said to Louise, "You looking so grown-up in your swimsuit. I know the boys in the village have a lot of talk about which of the girls they waiting to deflower, but they all know that they can't even look at you too hard because they would not live to see the light of day. I am here to protect you from all of these thugs. You would not realize it but all of these young boys try with as many girls as possible. It is like a competition to see who could score the highest number. They know how I feel about that so they would not dare try that with you."

On their way home from the beach, Oswald stopped and purchased two snow cones. He gave one to his sister and said, "Sis, I don't want to repeat myself, but I am so proud to have a sister looking like you. You are our princess. All of us feel the same way about you.

We never thought that we would have a sister so 'red. Everyone talk about your 'good' hair and what a nice complexion you have and that it is so pretty." Louise repeated what she had been saying for as long as she could remember, she sucked her teeth, said "I don't know what is the big deal about my color, because I don't feel pretty or different from you all. I am just like everyone else." Oswald responded, "Well, you would never realize what we are talking about because the truth of the matter is you do not live in our skin. That is why you take your beauty for granted. If you were our color and had our 'hard' hair, then you would realize what I am talking about." Louise quickly said, "Okay, Ossie, that's enough about me now." They both continued their leisurely walk until they reached home.

Naomi was now home from work and was in the tiny kitchen preparing dinner on the kerosene oil stove. The dinner consisted of stew potatoes and corned beef with flour gravy; added for flavor was some mellow cream butter. They both ate hungrily, finishing off with some *mauby* drink.

Louise and all her siblings were now at home, chatting about everything and everyone in the village. Louise's brother Fred talked about some of the "worthless girls" in the village—how he was so glad that his sisters were not like them. He just went on and on.

The night went by rather quickly, and in no time, it was 9:00 p.m. Naomi had her wash up, and then said that she was going to bed. She suddenly asked the children, "Wait, anybody see Geoffrey today?" None of the children had seen Geoffrey the entire day. Naomi, practically muttering to herself, said, "Strange, I hope he is all right."

It was now Wednesday. In a strange sort of way, Louise was looking forward to seeing Geoffrey. She thought to herself, *"I hope that there is nothing wrong with him."* Most of the day was practically uneventful for everyone in Naomi's household. It was a very hot summer's day, hotter than the day before. Maybe that explained why everyone stayed indoors, apart from Naomi who had to be out in the field working. Crop time had long passed, but she still had to work on the plantation, digging yams, potatoes, cassava, and eddoes. That was very much the norm after the reaping of the sugar canes, which involved the loading of the canes on the trucks. Naomi much preferred this type of work. For her, much less stress. Her whole body would ache after loading canes. This was actually like a 'picnic' when compared with that exercise. Naomi's day in the field ended about 5:30 p.m.

It was now 7:00 p.m. On the dot, the door handle turned, and there, to everyone's surprise, was Geoffrey. Geoffrey looked very clean shaven. Even his attire looked fresher than usual, and he also smelled of cologne. Naomi teasingly said, "Geoffrey, how you looking so good though? Like you had a date." Geoffrey, smiling broadly, said to Naomi, "But why you don't give me a break? A man can't dress up sometimes? He shouldn't look the same way all the time, you know?" Naomi looked at him lovingly and said, "I only teasing you. You were only away for a day, and all of 'we' missed you." Geoffrey responded and said, "Well, I very glad to hear that because you all 'is' my family—I love all of you." Geoffrey inwardly scolded himself for that lie. He knew within his heart that the only reason he was there was to be close to Louise. Geoffrey tried to stay away yesterday and succeeded, but when he thought of the great pleasure that he got from Louise the night before, he knew he had to come back and be there to see her again. Geoffrey knew that it would only be a matter of time when he would succeed in having her all for himself, which was when everyone else had fallen asleep.

By 8:00 p.m., and getting impatient as only Naomi had retired to bed by then, he said, "Louise, we going to play some cards tonight, Okay! When you are ready, just tell me." Louise responded, "Okay, uncle, whenever you are."

By 9:30 p.m., everyone else had gone to bed, and their card games were now well underway. Geoffrey, with excitement in his voice, said to Louise, "Let me get your basin of water now, and you go wash up. You know I don't like you washing up too late because you might get too tired and then unable to do so." Louise agreed, saying, "Yes, Uncle."

As Louise proceeded to wash up, Geoffrey again got an eyeful by ensuring that the makeshift door from the shed roof leading to the kitchen was slightly ajar while Louise was washing up. After changing into her nightgown, she again sat next to Geoffrey and continued with their card game. Geoffrey had earlier taught her how to play another game by the name of Suck Me Well. She enjoyed the game but innocently asked Geoffrey, "But why that name for this game?" Geoffrey, with a broad smile on his face, said, "Well, Louise, you would not understand, but that is the additional fun we are going to have tonight because tonight I want to reverse what we did the other night and, well, basically incorporate more." Louise looked at Geoffrey, puzzled. He said, "to break it down for you, I will be your lollipop tonight, and tonight I will not only be your lollipop, but I would need to add a bit more fun to our game." Geoffrey gave Louise some instructions as to what he wanted her to do. Louise looked up at Geoffrey in astonishment and said, "But uncle, I do not understand what you are trying to say, and I am scared!" With that Geoffrey said while placing his arms around her, "Louise my precious angel, I am your protector, I will never harm you in any way, besides it is just a fun game." After that remark, Geoffrey momentarily proceeded to tickle her around her neck and under her arms at a fast pace, causing her to laugh out loudly and uncontrollably. Louise said, "Please stop! Stop! Uncle, please." Now giggling nervously at that point. Geoffrey said, "Okay my princess, enough of that. Calm down my dear, you are going to be alright, trust me." However the pervert of a man Geoffrey did not stop there, after trying to calm Louise down for approximately ten minutes, he then proceeded to kiss her on her lips; and simultaneously touched her inappropriately, while telling her, "Louise you are special and beautiful and you will never know how happy you make me." He reminded her that it was just a fun game and that it was their little secret.

Chapter 15

THE INAPPROPRIATE TOUCHING continued almost nightly during Louise's vacation, after everyone had retired to bed. Some nights, Geoffrey would reverse the process. In his own words, he would say to Louise, "This makes it more exciting for both of us."

One night during one such inappropriate touching Geoffrey jumped up from the position he was in and asked Louise suddenly, "But Louise, you start to see any 'changes' yet?" While explaining in more detail what he meant. Louise tried to explain that there were 'changes' but it was not the case every month yet and that her mother had told her that it would eventually happen every month.

Geoffrey remained standing while telling Louise that she should remain in the position that she was in. He said, "I am not going to harm you okay? Trust me, you are my princess. I would never harm you." This pedophile for a man on this occasion with his heinous and depraved mind had already decided that he wanted to get 'lucky'. He started to playfully stroke the palm of Louise's hand, reminding her that he would never harm her and that she was indeed his precious little angel. He appeared a bit nervous, but then as he did on the previous occasions kissed her on her lips instead of her cheek, while touching her inappropriately. Eventually the 'scumbag' he is, took his sickening thoughts/acts a step further by violating Louise's body.

Louise became very alarmed at this stage, and started sobbing uncontrollably. Geoffrey, at this point like a typical child molester used reversed psychology on her while placing his hand over her mouth to muffle her cries said to her, "Louise my dear child. Everything is going to be alright." He continued, "Louise you know that you all lives have improved substantially since I came into the picture. You must believe me that I care about your welfare and will not harm you in any way." He added, "And Louise, I will reward you big tonight, so don't worry my angel. You have done extremely well, and you will be fine, I assure you."

Geoffrey went on and on, continued using the typical grooming behavior of a child molester, reminding her that if her father had cared about her, he would at least have been there for her financially and otherwise; and that he Geoffrey has been fulfilling that role. He again reminded her that it was their 'big' secret and that she should tell no one, that if she does, both of them would be in 'big' trouble.

Geoffrey then quickly got up. He said, "Louise I will pour some water from the pipe in the basin. Please wash up again. I will help you with that process." Geoffrey as quietly as possible got the water from the pipe in the yard, and instructed her to wash up as quickly as possible. After she completed this exercise, Geoffrey said to her, "I have to leave now. Go get some rest." As an afterthought, Geoffrey said, "Here take this bonus of fifty dollars, which would enable you to buy whatever you want tomorrow. Okay."

Louise watched as he reinforced the door. He then whispered to her, "Have a good night, my princess."

The incestuous relationship with Geoffrey and Louise continued from that point onward throughout the summer. During that period, Geoffrey even experimented with different situations. He would always tell her that he would be gentle and that it was more exciting to change the positions. He would always remind her that the money he had been giving her would never have been forthcoming otherwise. There were times, during the final days of her vacation, when Louise wanted to 'open up' and talk to someone. She thought of possibly talking to her brother Ossie about what was happening, but she decided against it, fearing that Ossie would go ballistic and harm Geoffrey; and that Ossie would go to jail, and she would not have him in her life. Louise had become so confused about the whole situation that there were times too when she still looked up to Geoffrey as her protector, but other times, she was really angry, hurt, frustrated, and felt very lonely and sad. A total mixture of emotions.

Louise also, on some occasions, harbored the resentment she felt toward men in general as a result of what had been taking place over the summer. Other times, she tried her best to rationalize that Geoffrey had given her so much monetarily and that, were it not for him, she would not have been able to buy cream for her face and skin and other toiletries in general. Having him in her life meant that there was now a certain degree of independence, being able to have access to cash. She was well aware that her mother would never have been able to do so because of her mother's state of poverty.

One day, while Louise sat quietly with a blank stare on her face on the front doorstep, which was a piece of stone almost rectangular in shape, Ossie looked at her and told her that he had noticed a change in her. He tried but failed to get into Louise's thoughts. She just would not budge. Ossie even asked her if her period was making her unwell and if by chance that was the cause of her mood swings. Louise shook her head and told her brother, "I will be all right, so please do not worry about me. I just want to be left alone." Ossie said, "Okay, if you say so," And walked off. He quickly turned back and said, "But, remember I am here for you. I will always be here for you, and you know that too. I want to see that beautiful smile on your face again. The way you smile, you always light up this house—such a wonderful smile. Promise me that, whatsoever is bothering you that you will get it out because only if you do so are you going to get the problem solved." Louise repeated that she wanted to be left alone.

Chapter 16

THE VACATION HAD ended. the new term was upon Louise. Louise tried her best to concentrate on her schoolwork, but the more she tried the more difficult a task it appeared to become. She would always have these visions of Geoffrey violating her body. These visions sometimes made her literally sick to her stomach.

Her teacher noticed that her grades were beginning to fall, that she was withdrawn and appeared to have much difficulty concentrating on even simple tasks.

The situation had gotten very bad in the classroom for Louise, and her grades had now fallen from straight As to Ds in many cases as most of the time Louise would place her head on the desk and fall asleep.

Louise's mother was summoned to the school to speak with her year head. The year head is the teacher responsible for the specific year group. After an extensive interview, Louise bluntly refused to open up about what was bothering her and continued to suffer in silence.

One evening Louise met Geoffrey some distance away from the school's gate as she had indicated earlier that she wanted to meet with him and reiterated, "But not at my mother's house." Geoffrey appeared with a broad smile on his face for the meet but quickly became serious as he realized that Louise was not smiling.

Louise gave Geoffrey a good telling-off. She told him that he had messed up her life and that she did not ever want to see him again. And that he must stop visiting her mother's house. She also said to him, "I know my rights, this is child abuse! You were supposed to be my protector, but you did the reverse. You have caused my personality, my grades, my everything to become so messed up that I cannot even think straight. Oh! How I hate you! And all men now with intensity because of you."

Geoffrey tried to calm her down and also tried to be apologetic. He attempted to place his arms around her. Louise shrieked, "Stop it! Do not touch me. You make me feel like I want to vomit."

"You are also a fucking pedophile. You came into my mother's life pretending that you had the welfare of all of us at heart, but you had your own agenda. You are also a fucking scumbag, who should be placed in a garbage dump. You have not only violated my body in the worse possible way but you have left me with scars that will be very difficult to erase." She pointed her finger in his face and continued said, "You should be glad that I do not have a car and cannot drive, because your ass would be on the ground all like now dead."

Her anger at what he had done to her was beyond intense. She jumped up suddenly and slapped him in his face on the left and right cheek at least three times on each cheek, while hyperventilating at the same time. He winced, and touched his cheeks as if in pain from the intensity of the slaps. He quickly regained his composure.

Geoffrey lingered and appeared worried. He said to her that he was very sorry and sad about what he had done—that he felt ashamed of himself and that he would do anything to make her feel better. He said, as per her wishes he would not come to her mother's house again. Geoffrey also proposed paying her for all the pain and suffering she was experiencing. He pleaded with her not to take it any further as he would be in big trouble. She also said to him "You fooled me all along and told me that 'we' would get into trouble. Who is 'we'? You mean you."

Louise turned away but then looked back and said, "About the payment, I will let you know about that very, soon." Geoffrey was amazed as to how grown-up Louise appeared now, that she seemed more streetwise, and he hoped and prayed that she would not cause him to be reported to the authorities by telling her mother or her teachers at school.

Geoffrey said, "And Yes! About the payment, please let me know how much very soon. Again, I am sorry about everything. I wish I could erase that from our memories. I was really stupid and selfish. I messed up big-time." His apologies did not cut it. Louise looked at him with much disdain while saying to him, "Leave! And leave right now!"

Two days later in the afternoon. She did not attend school that day. She phoned Geoffrey, and literally shouting said, "Hello Mr. Pedophile! I must have **no less** than eight hundred dollars per month. The time and place just after 3:00 p.m. a few yards away from my school." Geoffrey at the other end, with head down, shaking it from side to side replied, "That is alright with me, I will deliver as promised." Louise still livid shouted in a threatening tone of voice said, "You better had, if not you know what is coming." He responded, "I understand! I give you my word." Thereafter, she quickly slammed down the phone in his ear. He briefly held the phone to his ear as if in a trance, before placing it back on the receiver.

Chapter 17

THE YEAR WAS 1969. Louise had just completed her secondary education. Louise never regained the enthusiasm for her schoolwork and life in general after that period of abuse at the hands of Geoffrey. Neither did she disclose to anyone what had actually transpired. She was still beautiful but now had a reckless streak in her personality and how she viewed life in general and her hatred for men intensified. One thing she was happy about was that she had made Geoffrey pay her a sum of money monthly.

Shortly after her seventeenth birthday at home and alone, Geoffrey contacted her on the phone. He said to her, "How are you?" Louise sucked her teeth and responded, "How am I my ass! What is your fucking problem now?" He in a very subdued tone of voice said to her, "I can no longer afford to pay you that sort of money on a monthly basis…. Besides you are now seventeen and…………

Before he was able to continue, Louise interjected, with much anger, literally shouting "And what? I am now at the age of consent right. Listen! I don't give a fuck about you. Your money can never erase the mental anguish that I have suffered because of you. On hindsight, my only regret is that your ass was not in jail all like now serving a long time for rape." She slammed the phone down in his ear. Her mother Naomi was never able to find out the reason why Geoffrey suddenly stopped seeing her.

Naomi muttered to herself, *He must have picked up with a better-educated or better-looking woman than me. I know he was too good to be true. I should have known that it would come to an end sooner rather than later—that is just my luck. I know I am ugly and should have been glad that he stayed around for as long as he did. Poor Louise, I feel more for her than for myself because at least she had a father figure in her life who I know she loved dearly and whom she looked up to.*

Naomi realized that Louise did not ask any questions as to why Geoffrey was no longer visiting. She was glad in a way that Louise did not. Naomi really felt like a big failure, as she often tried to shield Louise from negativity and was always very protective of her children. Louise especially when it came to a father figure in her life. She muttered to herself *Well, at least I am glad that she has not asked about his sudden departure.* However, Naomi thought that Louise was acting strange and that more than likely the reason for that was that she was pining over Geoffrey's sudden disappearance from the household.

She dared not broach the subject because she did not want to appear to be a total failure. Naomi muttered to herself, *"At least I have my pride, and I really don't want Louise to feel badly that Geoffrey has abandoned her mother. I will deal with it if she questions me. If she doesn't, I will keep my mouth shut."*

Chapter 18

A T SEVENTEEN WITH only two GCE certificates, which were English and Spanish, Louise registered and succeeded in getting a temporary job in a government department. She was able to purchase her own clothing for work and other essential supplies. She went a bit overboard with the makeup, miniskirts, and high heels at work. She, however, always wore a jacket to temper any 'over the top' comments from her supervisor or peers.

During this period, consciously or unconsciously Louise began prostituting herself for money with numerous men in a subtle and sophisticated way with no real love in her heart for them.

Louise was like magnet to the Barbadian men, everywhere Louise went, the men would follow her. They all wanted to date her. **There are so many that she slept with, she admitted that she had loss count of them.**

She learned the trick very early. Initially, she would go on a few dates with selected men and would appear to be a prude. When they made sexual advances to her and things started to get steamy, she would suddenly declare, "Oh, I do not go there. Besides, I have a headache" or "I am tired. I would rather be taken home." However, by date three, Louise's tune would change somewhat. In an alluring manner, she would captivate them in a suggestive way. **She always appeared to know the exact eroticism,** teasing them, and before their advances could go any further, Louise usually with a 'fake' smile, pointing downward at her privates, would say, "to get this, you must have the money to deliver, baby! No money, no sex" The 'lucky' ones she chose to sleep with always had to literally pay a price--in cash, of course--for her "prized" possession. This prostitution to a great extent appeared to be a reaction from the experience with Geoffrey which manifested itself in the form of very low self-esteem, and her hatred towards the opposite sex. Also, the fact that she never knew her father impacted greatly on how she viewed them. In her distorted and twisted emotional state, she believed it was 'pay back time'. After the sexual encounter with the individual man, on arrival home she would scrub her skin vigorously with a scrubbing brush until there was bruising, as in her words *to remove all of the 'filth of the bodily contact, with all of these stupid ass men.* Her first serious relationship was with a man some fifteen years her senior. Michael was tall and dark.

It was Saturday night, Louise attended a party with her best friend Sue who was conservatively dress. As usual Louise was all dressed up This charming man approached her. He introduced himself to her said, "Hello my name is Michael." He examined her from head to toes, and then said, "You look so hot! Are you Barbadian? Or are you from over and away?" She responded, "First of all, let me introduce you to my best friend, Sue. He shook her hand, said "nice to meet you." Sue responded, "You too." Immediately after the introduction, Louise disconnects from Sue totally. All of her attention now focused on Michael. Sue shook her head in disbelief, stepped aside and exited.

In a suggestive flirtatious pose she said to him, "My name is Louise and No, I come from right her in good old 'Bim'. *(Barbados is often referred to as 'Bim')* He continued to undress her with his eyes and said "gosh man, you are as good as they come! Nice shape, nice 'boobs' and from what I see nice legs too" Spontaneously he said, "Turn around and let me get a full view. I want to see your backside too." Smiling, Louise complied and said, "All of this is mine." He continued with his admiration. He started stroking her hair and said, "Everything just right baby, and the most important thing for me you have and that is the color." Still smiling, Louise said "Thanks! And for your information, what you see is what you get." She added, "And by the way, you looking real cool and handsome too."

He now smiling and salivating said, "Well, all of the ladies tell me so." He focused again on Louise and said, "All of my dreams tonight are going to be about you. Girl, you rock my world. Please tell me you are at the age of consent. I have to make sure I am not breaking any law." She responded, "I can assure you that I am." He said "That sounds great." She said, "We have just met, but it appears as if you have ideas already." He stroked the palm of her hand and said, "Yes I do. I want us to be real friends." She looked at him intently and said, "You mean like girlfriend and boyfriend." He said, "I am so smitten by you that actually I do." She responded and said, "Maybe that can work, because I like you too."

The party was now 'kicking' with a mixture of music, but mostly suitable for lovers. They are on the dance floor. Michael held her closer and closer. By midnight, there was no space between them. Michael turned to Louise still holding her close said, "Let us go outside and get some fresh air. Besides, the moon is out, just perfect for lovers."

He led her outside to a secluded area. He undressed her with extreme passion. They made some "sweet" love. He said to her during the love making, "Open baby". She stared into his eyes, looked concerned said, "Do you have condoms? I want you to cover up." He did not want to do so. He placed his finger on her lips and continued. He reassured her and said, "No my angel. It's all right, don't worry my darling, I love you so very much and I know we are going to be together forever, and besides I cannot get women pregnant." Louise felt reassured hearing that statement and continued to enjoy the love making which culminated in the sex act.

From that night onwards, they continued with their love making sessions, he on all occasions repeated that he could not impregnate women, and would always insist on having unprotected sex. They just could not get enough of each other. Sometimes two and three times a day, especially on weekends.

Her mother eventually got word that Michael was actually a 'player'. She was livid. One afternoon while both Louise and her mother were at home alone, Naomi approached her. She told Louise that they must have a serious talk immediately. Louise acted surprised and impatient. She said to her mother, "What is this all about? And why do you have that angry expression on your face. Tell me now. Quickly! As I am leaving here shortly."

Naomi's anger was reaching 'boiling point'. She responded and said, "I will tell you now. It is about this big 'hard back' man Michael that I see coming her to you. I understand that he is fifteen years your senior. Everybody in this village telling me about all of the women he has; and what a no good person he is. They want to know what a pretty young girl like you doing with him." Her mother was up in her face, continued, "every time I look around he is up behind you. Some nights when I am trying to get a rest, he is with you outside of my house all sorts of hours. I know that you all must be out there having sex, because all of that noise I am hearing cannot be footsteps or the neighbor's dogs howling."

Still extremely angry and also hyperventilating, Naomi continued "He is going to 'use' you and when he gets tired with you, he will dump you." Louise frowned and said, "What is the big deal anyway?" Her mother responded, "What is the big deal. I did not raise you like that."

"Another thing, I understand from reliable sources that you are dealing with lots of different men too on the side for money. Don't you know that is prostitution? Where is your sense of self-worth?" Louise placed her arms around her mother, and said, "Please do not worry about me. I assure you that I will be alright." No amount of quarreling by her mother helped in dissuading Louise from this very toxic relationship. In fact, it appeared that the more her mother grumbled, the stronger the relationship grew. In a very short span of time, Louise started to get telephone calls from various women who 'cussed' her out, in some cases, telling her to leave their man alone. Louise confronted Michael on more than one occasion, asking him if he had been giving her telephone number to different women. His response was always that there was no way he would do something like that, so she should stop questioning him.

On one such occasion it was late afternoon. Louise was at home alone, the phone rang, Louise said "Hello", One of Michael's women was at the other end said to Louise "Why you don't leave my man alone?" Louise's response was, "Why you don't go and fuck yourself and stop harassing me!"

Louise also grew increasingly worried about his insistence on having unprotected sex. On each occasion, his response was always that in addition to him been unable to impregnate women, he liked the 'feel' so covering up was a no-no. She was in love and readily complied on every occasion. Toward the end of the year, with their relationship still going strong, Louise realized that she had missed her period by one week. Of course she was very alarmed but reckoned that her body might still be adjusting to its maturity. However, by day ten, Louise went into panic mode. She made an appointment to see a doctor. The appropriate test was done. That was the longest day of her life, waiting for the result and not sure what was really going down. Meanwhile, Michael tried to reassure her by saying "you good, 'man', I am confident everything is okay." The result came back two days later.

The result was positive. Louise instantly informed Michael. Michael went ballistic! He jumped up from the chair where he was sitting, said to her, "But Louise, why did you allow that to happen?" Of course, a big argument erupted. Louise said, "What did you tell me repeatedly? You seem to conveniently have a short memory. You fooled me all along about not being able to impregnate a woman." Louise was shocked at his response, shouting, he said, "I do not want a baby at this time, so you have to terminate it, because if you do not I will end our relationship."

After the heated exchange, Louise recognizing that he wanted to have no part of a baby, made an appointment with the doctor to terminate the pregnancy. The pain of the procedure was so intense and severe, that Louise screamed throughout the entire ordeal. When the doctor had completed the procedure, Louise was still so 'hyped up' that she was still screaming.

Ironically, in spite of the strain that had developed as a result of this event, Michael was able to convince Louise that she was the one for him and that they would be together forever. He was always able to charm and convince her, and in the end she would always agree to rekindle the affair. As far as she was concerned, Michael was the man for her.

The relationship continued and remained volatile mainly due to the many women that Michael was seeing and continued to see. However, it was like history repeating itself over and over again. During the ongoing relationship, she had terminated at least another five pregnancies, all in the early stages.

Sue, aware of all the heart ache and negativity that had been going on for some time between Louise and Michael, sat Louise down one day, and said, "I have no control over your emotions, but like I said before you are such a beautiful young lady why are you permitting yourself to be used by him so consistently. Where are the long term benefits to this affair? Why don't you get it? Bang! Bang! translates into pregnancies, abortions and diseases." Louise responded and said, "I understand where you are coming from but I will come to a decision when I am ready emotionally and otherwise, I know you care about my welfare, but just leave me alone, I will do what I have to in good time."

Sue spontaneously hugged Louise and said, "I am sorry if I came over too 'rough' but you know you have my back forever." Louise responded, "I know, and that is what true friendship is all about."

Some months later, with much reflection, and soul searching, out of the blue one day Louise arranged to meet Michael at her home. She told him that it was important that they meet right away. Michael was a bit apprehensive but agreed to do so. On his arrival Louise sat him down. She appeared very composed, said to him, "How are you?" Michael now grinning from ear to ear responded,

"Ready to make some sweet love to you as usual my darling." She, with a serious expression on her face replied "Oh really!" Michael at that point appeared a bit concerned asked her, "What is going on with you. You sound very 'stiff'. You are not pregnant again I hope." Louise shook her head and said "No. I am not." and with sarcasm said, "Aren't you happy to hear that?" He, with a smile on his face, and acting like a 'winner' sat upright, as if he wanted to jump out of the chair, and with much authority responded, "Of course I am, very happy. Actually elated, because you know you and I don't add up when it comes to that."

Louise became restless, and shifted her body on the chair, while shaking her head from side to side, stared intently at him, and in a measured tone said, "You know we have been having challenge after challenge in this relationship for a very long time right. To cut a long story short, this party is over!"

Michael with a very surprised look on his face jumped up from the chair, pointed at her privates, and said, "I thought you call me to give me some of that! You know that belongs to me!" She got up from the chair briefly and was in his face, said, "If you are not crazy I am. But then again, I know I am not. I am confident that I will find someone who respects me and cares for me."

She regained her composure, and sat. Michael became very upset, agitated and shocked at the same time, still standing shook his head and said, "Well! Well! Just like that. I hope you are not allowing your 'goody too shoes' friend Sue to influence you and causing us to break up. We have such a wonderful relationship, one that I cherish dearly and now this is how you 'do' me!" She was calm and collected and in a very determined tone of voice said, "Absolutely not this has nothing to do with Sue or anybody. This is about you and me. Please leave right now."

Michael knelt down in front of her, with a very sad look on his face, with hands clasp, said to her, "I beg you, don't dump me, I can't live without you. Please Louise, Please!"

He looked at her longingly, still kneeling, and shaking his head from side to side. Louise got up from the chair, opened the door said to him, "I say leave, and leave right now!" He took two slow steps towards the door, turned back and said to her, "But does this mean that I can still come around and get what is mine?" Louise ignored his statement and in a very assertive tone of voice said to him, "If you do not leave immediately I will call the police and have you arrested for trespassing."

Michael rolled his eyes like a lunatic, shook his head in disbelief and exited. Louise immediately slammed the door shut with a vengeance. He was kind of 'lucky', that he did not get an injury from the door in the process.

Shortly thereafter, Louise called her best friend Sue and asked her to meet her at Crystal Waters Beach Bar on the South Coast within an hour. Sue said to her, "Anything for you my dear friend, but it better be important because I cancelled my original plan to meet you there."

Within an hour they met as arranged, sat at a table after ordering two locally brewed Banks Beers. Sue said to Louise, "Okay why am I here?" Louise jumped up while moving her hips from side to side with 'belly dancing moves', chanted, "I dump his ass. Oh yes I did." Sue responded, "You talking about Michael or you are kidding me." Louise said to her with much jubilation, "Of course I have dumped his ass." Sue with a broad smile said to her, "You call that Woman Power! Finally!" Louise responded, "Yes indeed, finally!" They gave each other a "High Five." After which Sue said, "Hallelujah!" Louise responded, "Amen!" They both then "drank" to that.

One week later while at Brown's Beach in the parish of Saint Michael, Sue said to Louise, "I am still on a high as a result of your ability to finally dump that jack ass Michael, I have two questions to ask you, first one, please tell me, why did you remain in that toxic relationship for such a long time?" Louise replied, "You really want to know?" While smiling. Sue said, "But of course I do. I would not have asked you otherwise."

Louise became very demonstrative; she opened the palm of both hands very wide and said, "He is huge down there! I got a feeling of euphoria whenever he banged it." Sue shook her head from side to side, then said, "other question, Why did you continue to 'lay down' and get pregnant for him so many times? Once is a mistake, but more than once is a habit." Louise said, "All I can tell you, apart from the euphoria when he is banging it; around my unsafe period, I always insisted that he 'pull out' just before he reach his plateau. Guess I was unlucky on many occasions. Looking back now I should have insisted on him covering up every time. The other thing, I was so hyped up during those moments he probably did not 'pull out' at all, and I did not realize it. He would have done something like that, knowing him. Girl! His love making technique was so hypnotic it is indescribable. Anyway, he is a dog and should have been in the dog house a long time ago."

Chapter 19

S HORTLY AFTER THE breakup Louise was able to secure a job in a private firm as personal assistant to the manager, with a substantially higher pay than her job in government. She was happy that she was able to type accurately and fast, that she had learned speed writing, and that she had some knowledge of accounts even though she acknowledged that she must pursue the Ordinary Level certification in accounting so that she could be more marketable.

She immediately arranged to meet Sue. At the meet she said, "I want to share some good positive news with you. Remember the job I told you that I had applied for; well the General Manager called me yesterday and said that I am successful, so I get to start next week. All of the terms and conditions are better, plus I think I need a new scene anyway as I am getting bored as hell in this government job." Sue responded with excitement, "Very nice, I am happy for you. That new job should help you to remain focus." Louise quickly responded with a broad smile said, "Focus on what? More men or no men." Sue, while laughing said, "You are just too much."

Louise continued to get all the attention and more from the opposite sex. The local Barbadian men who came in contact with her were all captivated by her beauty, 'red' skin, and lovely hair by cultural standard.

Particularly back then, and still today, many Barbadian men classify beautiful women based on these characteristics.

One day, while out for lunch with Sue, Louise said, "Oh Lord, Sue, these men got my head confused and tied up! I wish they would stop coming on to me. Everywhere I turn the same story. Right now I have to make up my mind with regard to at least five different men that I am looking at in a serious way that would not stop confusing me. My boss too. He is coming on to me every day, day in and day out. I have to make the right decision."

Sue responded, "don't forget, you look different from most of we 'Bajan' women. You real lucky, I wish I were in your shoes." Louise said, "Yeah, this is bare stress! I think you better off than me." However, Sue insisted that Louise was the lucky one. "But," Sue said, "and this is a big but, you don't think that dealing with all of these different men is gross disrespect and an insult to your mother?" Louise gave Sue a nasty look and said, "Insult, disrespect--you better come again. My mother had us from six different men who abandoned all of us, and of course, there were other no good men in her life, I can attest to one especially who is a real scum bag. So don't go there at all. Furthermore, with regard to trying to make up my mind, if by a certain time I can't make up my mind as to which of these fellows I want, I may very well take on all, and Sue, that is the truth, between you and me."

Sue said, "But, Louise, that is a lot of men--too many, by any standard." Louise responded, "You hear what I tell you. I have to try to make up my mind because as far as men are concerned, I can't take any of them anyway. I hate all men; they are just a bunch of stupid ass men! So who cares? We shall see what we shall see, okay." She continued, "In any event, I demand payment from all of them but in a passionate and seductive way, so what is the big deal? It is an exchange, remember, an exchange!" While gesturing with her right thumb and index finger. Louise quickly added, "But, Sue, just remember that this is between us, okay. Because some 'Bajans' real malicious and I don't want any of them to know my business." Sue said, "I understand, but just be careful, your safety is of the utmost importance to me."

A few weeks passed by and Sue had not seen Louise or heard from her. When she finally did, Sue said, "I was so worried about you, what happened?" Louise responded, "What happened? First of all, I was very, very busy doing my own thing." "And what might that be?" Sue asked. Louise said, "Well, I had such a blast that I am now literally worn out. Remember I told you about these five 'potentials,' I was able to pull it off during those weeks that you hadn't seen me, and to tell you the truth, I scored big-time. I even got a bonus because--remember I told you that my boss kept coming on to me? I finally made out with him too. I made more money during that period than what I get paid monthly from my salary, and you know my salary is not small. You can call it being greedy if you want to, but what the heck, I do not care."

Sue got extremely intense and said, "Tell me about it. Give me the rundown because this 'in' sounding right." Louise said, "Sue you know why it 'in' sounding right to you, because you 'does' pretend that you are so righteous, but for me, it is reality." Sue responded, "Well, Louise, talking about me being righteous to each his own. If that is the kind of life you enjoy, well that is great. But tell me how you managed?" Louise responded, "What you really mean? You mean literally taking on all of them, or how I manage to arrange the whole thing without any suspicion from any of them?" "Of course the suspicion part, because I am not interested in the details of your sexual escapades because it just don't sound right to me," Sue said. Louise while smiling, responded, "It was much easier than I anticipated because when I went out with Mr. X one night, I just tell the others that I had a very busy schedule at work and had to work late, so I would not be available.

They all understood because, really and truly, I am now trying to get to know them anyway. Besides, I had a--well you can call it a calendar, but it was simply a notebook with the names and dates." Louise laughing again, and with a bit of arrogance said, "As for my boss who kept annoying me, I saved him for last. I told him for that entire period prior to his date that I was having some really bad headaches, and he believed me because during the day, I played the part very well." Sue simply looked at Louise, as if trying to come to grips with what Louise had just enunciated, while saying, "Well, well, only Louise could pull off something like this."

Louise was indeed very proud of her achievements. Thanks to all these men, she was now renting her own apartment, and as for clothes, Louise's wardrobe was now so full of clothes and shoes that she barely had space to add more to her collection, but she continued. Shopping for Louise was very addictive, especially since she had gotten the chance to go to Miami on one occasion, New York on another, and more recently, London. Louise, on her trips, would go into the malls, especially the big department stores and spend the entire day shopping, buying up as much designer wear as she could. She often said while shopping, "Like I going to shop till I drop." As she put it, "I now have the travel bug, thanks to all of these stupid ass men!" Sue said, "But wait a minute, why do you constantly refer to them as 'stupid ass men', and yet you keep lying down for them, that does not make sense to me. Why?" Louise responded and said "Because as I told you on more than one occasion, I hate all of them." Sue said, "That still does not make any sense." Louise sucked her teeth, said, "I guess. Look! Stop confusing me right now. Are you a judge?"

Sue responded, "I wish I were a psychiatrist." Louise sucks her teeth again. Sue gave Louise a hug, and said, "I see you are getting very agitated so let's talk about this another time." Louise said, "Great!" Louise continued her escapades. Two years had now passed. Sue remained Louise's best friend throughout that period. Louise liked Sue very much. As she would tell Sue, "I like you because you are not too judgmental, at least most of the times, and thanks for being my friend because it is hard to find a true friend who would not go behind your back and talk bad things about you."

Of all the men in Louise's life, she took a fancy to Mark. For whatever reason, Mark made her heart skip a beat whenever they were together. For her, this was a strange phenomenon because, while going through the exercise with most of them, she often felt like she wanted to vomit and, in one or two cases, had to calm herself as she would have the urge to just jump up midstream.

One day, Louise telephoned Sue and asked Sue to meet her in the evening at 5:00 p.m. at her apartment, as she wanted to discuss an urgent matter with her. Sue agreed to do so, and arrived promptly at 5:00 p.m. At the onset of their meeting, Louise was very collected but appeared a bit nervous. Sue said to Louise, "Why am I here, I am anxious to know." Louise took a deep breath and said, "I have messed up big-time." She added, "You know I like Mark a lot, I mean a real lot."

"Yes," said Sue. Louise continued, "Well, to cut a long story short, I missed my period by a week. I always have unprotected sex with Mark, but, and this is a big but, in the heat of the moment, I had unprotected sex with one other guy, and in the case of another we had an 'accident' basically, and although he was covered up, because of the accident, well the 'thing' came off during the process. All of these situations occurred within days of each other. I am now not sure, one, if I am pregnant and two, who I am pregnant for. If I knew for sure that it was Mark's baby, that is, if the test is positive, I would keep it, but with these other guys in the picture whom I have no interest in whatsoever I now have a predicament in my hand."

Sue thought for a moment and tried not to come over as being punitive because she knew that Louise counted on her for sound advice, and additionally, Louise knew Sue always tried to bring calm to any bad situation. Sue said, "Well try not to worry too much but as you know, the first thing would be to find out if you have in fact been impregnated. After that, then we will talk some more about it." Sue asked, "How soon are you going to get the test done?" Louise responded, "Well, like yesterday, I guess." Sue said, "Okay, after that we will see what the best case scenario is, but you do know how I feel about abortions, right? You do know that I am a believer in pro-life?" Louise responded, "Yes, good old righteous Sue." They both had a little laugh at that statement to lighten things up a bit, but they both knew it was not funny. Sue said to Louise, "I would advise you to say nothing to any of these three men, not even Mark." Louise responded, "But of course I will not. I am not stupid." The result was back in a short time and revealed what Louise knew all along, that it was positive. Louise did not consult Sue, she went into panic mode, and said to herself, *I wish I could tell Mark. I wish it were his baby.* But reality stepped in.

Louise made the appointment with the doctor and did what she had to do discreetly. Of course, she always took along some pain killers. She vowed that she would not want to experience such severe pain ever again, as happened during her first termination of pregnancy. "She said to herself *"I am wiser, and I will only endure such intense pain if I were in labor and was having Mark's baby.*

Six weeks later Louise called Sue and asked her to meet her at Crane Beach, in the parish of Saint Philip, at 10:00 a.m. the following day. Sue of course agreed. While sitting on the sand on their beach towels, Sue said to Louise, "When you called me I swear you were overseas. What happened, were you pregnant? Because you did not get back to me." Louise said, "I am sorry that I did not get back to you." In response to your question, Yes! I was pregnant and I did what I had to do and terminate it." Sue became very agitated, touched her stomach area said, "Gosh, terminate. Again! Every time you call that word I feel sick to my stomach."

Louise in a pensive mood shook her head and said, "I really need to pull back on these escapades. I know that not only my body, but my soul needs some time to heal. I done having sex with these different stupid ass men for money and 'stick' with Mark. He is a good man."

Sue responded, "That is exactly what you should have been doing ever since. If you had done so you would not have been in that predicament."

Surprisingly, Louise jumped up, her demeanor changed, she said to Sue, "But wait a minute, I like I stupid. I am talking about having sex with Mark only, but I forgot my boss. I will continue to have sex with Mark, and my boss. I cannot leave him out just yet."

Sue shook her head in disbelief and said, "Sometimes, your personality is too distorted for me to understand. To say you love Mark, but yet you want to continue the affair with your married boss is absurd." Louise responded, "Okay! Give me a break; I will give continuing to seeing my boss some more thought. Are you happy to hear that now?" Sue responded, "My dear that is entirely up to you, because I am of the view that you have a love hate relationship with all men period." They departed shortly after wishing each other good bye.

Chapter 20

A YEAR HAD PASSED, and Louise continued to see Mark even though she continued to have the occasional rendezvous with Mr. Winters, her boss, who was an expatriate and who was married to a local black woman.

Louise could never understand why someone as handsome as he would marry 'that' person," as she always referred to his wife in this manner. "Maybe it was because he wanted status to remain in Barbados. I can think of no other reason," Louise resolved that she would try not to accede to his usual request for 'favors' as often as before even when he presented himself with all his charm, but of course, she had to continue. She could not refuse him totally because he treated her very well not only financially but otherwise, and he made her feel special, empowered and she did have a measure of love for him, at least sometimes. With such a big staff, she was singled out for special treatment. She actually felt proud of her achievements. As a matter of fact, Louise was promoted and given the title assistant manager, operations. A few staff members congratulated her from the get-go; others were more disingenuous, especially the female members of staff. Did Louise care? Absolutely not! As far as Louise was concerned, many a night when the female staff members; especially those who showed the most envy, were at home, she was there with her boss, working 'really hard', and she had to be rewarded big-time.

He was aware of her efforts to please him irrespective of his many challenges and his over-the-top sexual requests from her, as she often said to herself. How she always complied and performed was admirable as Mr. Winters knew that there was no way that his wife—who, as far as he was concerned, was a prude—would ever have complied. He once told Louise, "even whispering such to my wife would have caused much alarm and potential disquiet in the marriage." Louise just looked at him and smiled on that occasion while trying to unzip his pants.

Louise also traveled with Mr. Winters on many occasions, always telling Mark that it was business related. Mark, without knowledge of the true picture between Louise and her boss, was also happy for her when she announced the promotion to him. He told her that he always knew that she had it in her to be successful and that he was thankful that he had met her; that he loved her very much and had a big surprise coming her way. "That sounds interesting," Louise said. "I await this announcement with bated breath."

When Mark announced the news to Louise, it was a full moon–lit night. The sky was clear; even the stars were brilliant. It occurred in the patio of her apartment, which looked onto a well-kept lawn with miniature palm trees on both sides of the walkway and brilliant bougainvillea flowers in red and white. The ambience is so perfect for my announcement, Mark thought nervously. Mark had never felt this way before about any other girl.

Actually, Mark broke many a heart, girl after girl. It was addictive, but now Mark said, "This one is special, she is the one." Thoughts of spending the rest of his life with Louise consumed him. As far as he was concerned he was the luckiest man alive. Mark, being a true romantic, made the proposal to Louise at exactly midnight. When he showed her the sparkling diamond engagement ring, she was so emotional that she burst into tears. Mark went the traditional route.

He went down on his knee and asked her, "Louise, will you marry me?" Without hesitation, she said, "Yes! Mark, I will."

The wedding was set for a year later. While Louise was very happy and thrilled that she was now engaged to be married, there was still a measure of apprehension. Mr. Winters had fooled her into believing that one day he would leave his wife and marry her. As a result, Louise was not sure if she should keep her engagement to Mark a secret from Mr. Winters or allow her boss in on the engagement and accept any fallout that could follow. In any event, Louise had no intention of giving up the good life. She reckoned that even though she had given up her "services" with the other men, her boss was still very much a part of her life, still giving her extra cash. By any standard, it was quite substantial at times, and he also showered her with gifts no matter the occasion.

Louise eventually found the courage to tell her boss that she would be getting married to Mark. On that day she took a deep breath, then knocked on Mr. Winter's office door, entered and gave him a deep but tender kiss on the lips.

Mr. Winter said to her "Good morning my darling, your sweet kiss has brought me alive. I had a long night working on this project, the one I told you about." Louise said to him, "I hope it is coming along nicely. Boss, I want to talk to you briefly about some 'going' on in my personal life, which of course is part of yours."

With a radiant smile, she continued and said, so boss! Are you ready for it?" Mr. Winters with a twinkle in his eyes responded, "Yes! Tell me what you up to now." She proceeded to enlightening him at that point said, "Honey I know you talk about leaving your wife and marrying me in the near future. That is so sweet of you, but I am well aware that divorcing your wife here in Barbados could take a long time as the justice system can be very sluggish." She continued, staring into his eyes, and stroking his well kempt blonde hair. "Honey, remember the guy that I told you about, well he wants to get married to me, but before accepting the proposal, I have been giving our situation much thought as you are the greatest lover I have ever had!"

He became very aroused on hearing that statement, and touched the growing bulge in his pants. He got up from his chair. Louise then assumed a very provocative standing position in front of him, with her breasts push forward and her backside pushed backward. He drew her closer to him, at the same time breathing heavily, said, "I don't see why our situation should change. We can still continue like we have been doing since I hired you."

He then gave her a deep passionate kiss on the lips, placed his hand up her short skirt, pushed her G-string aside, fondled her vagina, squeezes her 'butt', smiling broadly while looking into her eyes said, "I want to have you forever! You are so sexy, and attractive, **I wish I could have you for breakfast, lunch and dinner.**" He unzipped his pants, pushed her gently towards the desk. She leaned against it for support. Breathing very heavily he said, "I am going to give you the wonderful banging that you and I deserve for the day." She laughed softly while he thrust deep inside of her. When done, with a smile on his face Mr. Winters said to her, "That was so awesome and hypnotic." She responded and said, "Oh yes it was.

Shortly thereafter, she re arranged her attire, smiled, exited his office, closing the door behind her.

The year was moving along swiftly, at least so Louise thought. It was almost time for her big day. Planning was well on the way. Louise had earlier informed Mr. Winters about the wedding date. Unknown to Louise, Mr. Winters was very relieved as he knew that there was no way that he would ever divorce his wife and marry her. Even though she made him happy, that to him was never an option, but in order to continue their affair, he felt that that was the honorable thing to say. Now he said to himself, *I can continue to eat my cake and have it too.*

A week before the wedding, Mark and Louise met with the parish priest, who counseled them both. The priest went on talking to them for quite some time. At some point, Louise wondered if he had heard bad things about her or if it was her imagination and maybe it was just a formality with all the couples who agreed to have him perform their marriage ceremony.

The one statement that stood out in her mind was when he spoke of indiscretions, stating that "if that has been or is taking place, now is the time that it should cease. Otherwise, it would not make sense getting married." He spoke in depth about the marriage vows and reminded them both that these vows were very sacred.

Naomi was very happy that her last girl child was getting a ring on her finger, as she put it. Neither she nor any of Louise's siblings were so fortunate. The entire village where Louise grew up was told of the pending wedding. Most knew that they would not be invited, but they all got the information regarding the time of the church wedding, as they all said they wanted to see Louise.

Some said, "She is going to make a beautiful bride." Louise, of course, had already traveled to Miami to secure a beautiful bridal gown for herself, and she had also purchased her attendants' attire, and also her mother's own. Her favorite brother, Oswald, had the honor of being the father giver. Sue was her maid of honor. Her sisters were the bridesmaids and Fred and Peter accompanied the two sisters. Louise's mother was so emotional when she watched her daughter walking down the aisle after the ceremony that she cried tears of joy.

In her illusionary world, Louise's mother, however wished that her father was there to be the father giver. It was a beautiful wedding. Both the church and the hotel where the reception was held were magnificently decorated with colors that were in sync with the bridal party's attire.

Chapter 21

LOUISE WAS NOW twenty-seven years old, having been married for more than a year now. From the onset, Mark wanted to start a family. Louise was not sure about that. She said that she wanted to have her freedom for a bit longer. In the end, Mark complied. One evening after work, Mark told Louise that something was bothering him, and he wanted to discuss it with her urgently. Mark proceeded and said, "I got some shocking news today from the guys [meaning his friends]." Louise was anxious to hear. She said, "What, Mark, what?" Mark proceeded to tell Louise how angry he was. He said that all of the boys were laughing at him, asking him how he could really marry that whore. They asked him if the beauty went to his brain and prevented him from thinking straight. They continued and also said to him, "If we could name one man that your wife has not slept with, we would give you five hundred dollar bills. We know she left the village and moved into her fancy apartment, but even the boys in the village had some too. So you could very well imagine that all of her big-up people that she has been associating with since leaving the village have been getting some too."

Louise, of course, denied all that was said about her. She told Mark, "That is so not true, Mark, can't you see that they are trying to break up our marriage? As for boys in the village, I swear I never ever looked at any of those scumbags, furthermore sleep with them." Mark looked at her straight in the eyes. "What about the upper-class men?" Louise said, "What about them?" Mark said to Louise, "Look, I finished playing games. I don't believe the part about the boys in the village, period, but as for the upper-class men, I am not sure, and right now, I really do not care." Mark, after pondering for a moment with his head down, suddenly looked at her tenderly and said, "You know something, you are my wife and I am still so in love with you, to hell with everybody else." With that, he lifted Louise up while saying, "Look! Let's go try making a baby." Mark persistently tried to impregnate Louise, but that was not to be. Meanwhile, Louise continued her rendezvous with her boss, Mr. Winters.

In addition, more new faces emerged in her life, all of whom used her body as a playground. Louise was now extremely discreet, as she knew that for Mark to discover her dark secret on his own was not an option. She in her naiveté, felt that she was able to convince Mark that what his friends had said was not true, but for him to actually discover first hand, her continuous rendezvous with men in general, she believe, would be catastrophic.

For whatever reason, Louise craved the attention; **the more men that begged her to sleep with them, the more powerful she felt**. Of course, the story was always the same. They had to pay her for the favors. To Louise, they were all a bunch of stupid ass men, and she reminded herself how she hated them all! Of course, Louise learned her lesson and now always insisted that they cover up just in case she became impregnated by anyone else, apart from her husband; even though within her heart she figured that it was not to be.

She felt that the battering her body had taken had really done her an injustice in this regard. The time when she was impregnated and did not know who the father was always stood out in her mind.

The other times that she was impregnated, she at least had an idea as to who the would-be fathers were. Not that it made a difference now, she thought. Louise tried to erase all these situations from her thoughts—situations that were really, really bad, she reckoned. Louise looked up in the air and said a silent prayer, *"Dear God, please forgive me. Please do not punish me anymore for these indiscretions.*

One or two females showed lots of interest in Louise also, wanting to make her their lover. However, Louise was never turned on by same-sex escapades. She once told a friend that she found it to be very revolting.

One evening as Louise walked up Broad Street in the main town, Bridgetown from her office after work, this female lesbian who was nicely dressed, wearing a white blouse, red and grey strip tie and black pants, tan shoes and hand bag approached her. She said to Louise, "You looking so beautiful and charming, I like you. Can I take you to dinner or anywhere else that would be of interest to you?" Louise 'sucked' her teeth' and with much indignation and scorn said to the lesbian, "Why all of you women coming on to me too? Same sex escapade! Woman I do not go there!" At the same time she gestures with her right hand pointing downward to her vagina and gave the lesbian a nasty look said, "I prefer by far what the guys have down there. So you like many others may as well quit wasting your fucked up time and my time too." She sucked her teeth again and walked off.

Cracks started to emerge in Louise and Mark's union. Mark was desperate to plant his seed, but that was not to be. When they went out they appeared as the perfect couple, but at home, Mark became easily agitated. The situation became so intolerable that there was weekly verbal abuse from him. It got more volatile as physical abuse had 'creeped' in. On occasions, Mark would strike her without giving a care as to where the strike landed. Most of the time, Mark aimed for Louise's face during these abuses. On one such occasion, Mark arrived home from work earlier than usual. No greetings whatsoever. Louise was in the living room watching one of her favorite programs on television. Mark reached for the remote turned the television off. She became very angry, jumped up and was in his face said, "Why did you do that? That is being so ill mannered and uncouth." Mark in her face, said to her "Say that again." Louise very agitated responded, "I can say whatever I want too, and you can't stop me." He gave her a nasty look, and said "Sluts should not be in a peaceful environment watching television. They should be out on the street looking for the next hook up." She attempted to continue to speak, but that angered him greatly, He slapped her very hard in her face. She gently patted the area, hoping that it would 'drown' the pain.

Surprisingly, he actually looked very concerned and alarmed. He held on to her saying "I am so sorry. I did not mean to hurt you. Come let's go make a baby." She had the courage to fight back on this occasion, responded and said, "Hell No!" He pulled her by one hand, trying to get her to the bedroom. She forcefully resisted by holding on to the edge of the table for support with the other. Surprisingly, he gave up and goes into the bedroom lies on his back and stared up at the ceiling with a blank expression on his face.

The nights Louise escaped were when she locked herself in the bathroom and slept there until morning. Louise began to wonder if Mark was a psychopath. Mark, on the other hand, was convinced that this resentment was a result of Louise's promiscuity, at least based on what the fellow had told him.

One evening his best friend Sam paid him a visit. He found Mark to be in a pensive mood, and in Mark's hand was a 750 ml bottle of locally manufactured pure white rum, a good part of which was in a glass which he constantly sipped. This to Sam was a surprise. Mark offered to pour some of the rum in a glass for Sam. Sam declined and with a puzzled look on his face Sam said to him, "How long ago have you been drinking and why?" Before Mark could respond, Sam said, "You see that drinking 'thing', that's not a good idea." Mark responded and said, "Depression I guess. It numbs the pain." He continued, "To this very day, my wife has still not been totally truthful about whether she has been allowing all sorts of men to get on top of her when I questioned her. If only we could have a baby, I know that would be good therapy and help with the preservation of our marriage."

"I can't believe that this is the woman that I once loved more than life itself. Right now I resent her so very much, that it is indescribable." Sam said, "My advice to you is, if you find that your marriage has broken down to a point whereby it cannot be salvage, you should first seek counselling and if that does not work, both of you should go your separate ways. This abuse 'thing is a No! No! If you continue to abuse her, you can get yourself in trouble with the law, so I beseech you. Please take my advice." The other problem we have here in Barbados is that many 'Bajan' men are too 'fast'. Once they see a beautiful woman, they don't care whether she is married or not. They are up behind her all the blasted time." Sam patted Mark on his back, said, "Anyhow I have to leave now, but you have to stay strong, and reframe from abusing her. Keep me posted. You are a wonderful person and I would hate things to spiral out of control. We will for sure keep in touch." Mark thanked Sam for his advice.

It was the fourth year of their marriage. No impregnation had occurred, and of course, the quarrels continued and as if the verbal abuse could not get any worse, the physical abuse also intensified.

Louise made all kinds of excuses when she was asked by coworkers and her boss about the bruises and what specifically was going on. Louise was in total denial; she would always respond and say, "I am okay, don't bother about me."

One night Mark cornered Louise in the kitchen. He dragged her to the bedroom, locked the door, and tore her robe and negligee off. She was totally nude. He began striking her all over her body including her head and face, with the 'head' of one of his belts like a lunatic, while calling her whore, bitch, slut and garbage. She screamed in pain, and pleaded with him to stop. Mark ignored her pleads for him to stop. She feebly tried to fight back, but was no match for her husband. That however angered him greatly and his beating of her intensified.

Louise eventually fell to the ground, curled up in a fetal position, tried to cover her head and face from the constant battering. He continued his onslaught. Eventually the beating stopped, but she was still on the ground. Mark was wearing 'heavy duty footwear. He however suddenly raised his right foot, kicked her in her face. She cried out in agony and pain.

The time was now approximately 11:00 p.m. Mark was still raging like a lunatic and extremely angry. He mumbled, "I am done with this marriage! I will shortly be presenting you with divorce papers." He hurriedly packed his personal belongs in two suit cases. With pants in hand, wearing only his shirt and boxer, slammed the main door of the apartment shut and got into his vehicle, drove off, speeding as fast as possible on his way to his parent home.

Louise meanwhile in severe agony and pain dragged herself to the bathroom, attempted to get up, but was having difficulty. She held on to the vanity, tried to examine in the mirror the condition of her swollen face, black and blue eyes, belt marks on her breasts and other injury about her body. She was very weak. She crawled to the medicine cabinet, swallowed two pain killers. However she quickly collapsed on the bathroom floor, groaning in pain. She eventually fell asleep from discomfort and exhaustion.

Mark arrived at his parents' home in the early hours of the morning, around 1:25 a.m. He hurriedly lifted the suitcases from the trunk. Dragged them to the main door. Unlocked the door, leaving the suitcases in the hallway. He hurried to his parents locked bedroom, banged on the door. His father jumped up, rubbing his eyes prior to opening the door, asked "Who is it." Mark responded and said, "Dad open the door quickly! I have a very serious problem to deal with."

His father opened the door, looked him up and down, and asked, "What happen to you? Why are you in a state of undress? Did a man catch you in bed with his wife?" Mark now in a panic state, responded, "No dad. It is worse than that! I 'lost' it and beat-up on Louise very badly. I am so scared, come and go back to my place with me please. She will need help." Mark's father with an alarmed look on his face hurriedly put on his shirt and pants, said, "What! Are you crazy? Why would you do something like that to your wife? Nothing justifies beating a woman." Mark said, "Just come Dad, time is of the essence." On arrival back at the apartment Mark with trembling hands unlocked the main door. However, he briefly looked down at himself, realized that he was still not wearing his pants, rushed back to the vehicle, fetched it and quickly pulled it up. He with father behind him hurried into the bedroom. However, he did not see Louise there. He rushed to the bathroom where she laid. He gently lifted her up, took her to the bedroom, and covered her naked body with her robe. After examining the extent of the injuries, tears settled in his eyes. His father tried to hold back his own tears on seeing the extent of the injuries inflicted by his son on his wife. He shouted, "Oh my God! I have raised a monster! Why, Mark. Tell me why! She can't remain here in this condition. We have to take her to the hospital emergency department."

On arrival, the doctor examined Louise, and she was checked in as a patient. The doctor asked Mark a number of pertinent questions, after ascertaining that he was the abuser. The doctor informed Mark that due to the extensive injuries, the Police Department had to be informed. He also informed Mark, that more than likely he would be charged for battery and serious bodily harm. Mark did not respond. He appeared as if in a trance, and shook his head from side to side continuously.

Mark was indeed subsequently charged for battery and serious bodily harm. Mark hired an attorney to act on his behalf. Meanwhile Louise remained hospitalize for six weeks.

Two weeks after discharge, Louise was able to return to work. On the first morning, while dressing, Louise looked into the mirror and spent some time applying foundation to hide some visible remaining scars in her face and on other exposed parts of her body, like her arms. The doctor had earlier told her, that some areas would take time, to heal, but that eventually she would be fine.

Louise eventually agreed to drop all charges against Mark. Instead she settled for a sum of money. When her best friend Sue inquired from her, why did she dropped the charges, her rationale for dropping the charges was that Mark was a good man who had loved her dearly, but became an alcoholic which impaired his judgement; and she was convinced that her life style, and deception triggered the dramatic turn of events of her marriage, which she believe could have been avoided, had she 'come clean', prior to the marriage. In addition, she said that Mark's parents were respectable people in the community and that they were kind to her from the onset. Mark later personally expressed his sadness for her pain and suffering due to his actions. At the time of his expressed sadness in person, Louise did not respond to him.

Louise however expressed her wish to allow the divorce proceedings to take place. They both agreed. With no accumulation of assets collectively, the divorce was quickly finalized through attorneys that each had hired.

Louise now approaching thirty-one years of age and single remained in the rented apartment which she shared with her now former husband. He of course sought living accommodation elsewhere. On reflection she so wished that she was able to grant Mark what he so desperately needed, which was to bear his child. She blamed herself for taking on so many men into her life in such a personal and private way. She knew she had become heartless toward the opposite sex as a result of the sexual molestation she endured, coupled with the fact that she did not know her father. She once told her best friend Sue, that she even hated to hear their voices.

Louise yearned for a new beginning in every way possible. After giving it much thought, she resolved that she would catch up on her GCE certification at Ordinary Level, after which she would apply to the local University in an effort to gain admission. The process with regard to the completion of her Ordinary Level certificates took one year, and another year was spent doing Advanced Level subjects in Economics and Accounting. Louise was initially accepted at the University through its distant-teaching program due to limited space at that time. She was however later accepted. As a result of working full time, she decided to study on a part-time basis at the University in the faculty of Social Sciences. She opted to do a major in Economics with a minor in Management.

Shortly thereafter, recognizing the length of time that Part-time studies required, she decided to meet with her boss to explain the schedule, and asked for time during the day to leave work early to attend the University on most days. He of course at that time was not aware of her challenge in this regard.

It was a new work week, a Monday. Her appointment with Mr. Winters was scheduled for 10:00 a.m. Louise knocked and entered and sat in the chair facing her boss. On seeing Louise, Mr. Winters' eyes literally lit up. With a radiant smile on his face he said to her, "How are you my Dear? Come closer to me." Louise beaming now with excitement gets up from where she was seated, and sat on the edge of his desk facing him, and playfully touched his hair. She wore a very short skirt which exposed a significant amount of her thighs and underwear, leaving nothing to the imagination. She explained to him her rationale for asking for permission to attend classes at the University during the day. She said, "If I am able to leave work early most evenings, I get to graduate sooner. Do I have your permission?"

Mr. Winters was so excited to see her, he got up from his chair and went very close to her. He 'planted' a deep and long kiss on her lips while fondling her nipples. He then placed his hand far up her skirt and fingers her vagina, while saying, "You are so damn irresistible. Of course you can leave early every day if you wish. You have contributed greatly to my stay here in Barbados at all levels." Still fingering her, he placed her hand on the bulge in his pants, said to her, "Look! See what you have done to me. I don't want to appear to be too 'greedy' but am I going to get some of this tonight?" With a broad smile on her face she responded, "But of course, your wish is my command. You know I have never refused you making love to me, any time and any place." With a twinkle in his eyes, he continued fingering, and started breathing heavily said, "I am so horny for you right now, I wish I could lock the door and take it now, but I have a scheduled meeting soon."

Louise smiling said, "Taking it now is fine with me but I understand." She got up to leave. He pulled her back, said, "No stay!" He pointed down at his bulge again, told her "Look! He can't wait, so let the meeting wait". He quickly locked his office door, and lifted her on the desk and gently at first glided deep inside of her.

When done he gave her a deep kiss on the lips, after which he said, "As I said a few minutes ago, I am not a greedy person, but what about later tonight? Louise said, "Again!" He said, "why not? Don't forget I will be 'getting' less of you just now." She pondered briefly, and then responded, "Okay! If you insist." He squeezed her butt, gave her another deep kiss, after which she straightened her clothing, exited and closed the door behind her.

Her boss, allowing her to take time off whenever she had day classes was a huge advantage, as other students Louise spoke to found studying and not being given time off from their employer when necessary during the day to be quite challenging. However, Louise was now so busy that she rarely entertained Mr. Winters as she did previously. Mr. Winter was very understanding and was eternally grateful for whatever time she was able to give him for his pleasure. Louise was still beautiful, and she was able to purchase all and more, that were necessary to keep her looking good, thanks in part, of course, to Mr. Winters, who continued to shower her with money and gifts. Louise was still tempted to have affairs with other men who fancied her in a big way. She tried her utmost to remain focused on her studies and graciously declined, as she put it, "I am not ready for that now."

However, Louise knew that her sophisticated rendezvous with several different men was addictive and that the hiatus was, more than likely very temporary. In a short span of time, Louise would arrange dates, and just before the scheduled time, she would reluctantly make excuses in most cases. However, in some cases she willingly gave in, especially when the cash appeared attractive enough to be worth her time. As time went on, Louise forced herself and eventually made a pact with herself that she would remain resolute in attaining her goal of becoming a university graduate, instead of continuing with her sexual escapades.

Chapter 22

THE MORATORIUM CEASED when she met Ray. Raymond was pursuing graduate studies in psychology at the University of the West Indies, Cave Hill, where she was pursuing her undergraduate degree. He was born and raised in America, of Barbadian parentage. He was five years Louise's senior. Never been married and with no children of his own. The chemistry was so strong that they made passionate love almost instantaneously. However, Ray would always stop short of entering into her. Louise was slightly agitated at times about this state of affairs. This was really a first such encounter for her as previously, before you could say "jack robin," other men she encountered would try to achieve that objective.

Louise was so excited having met Ray, she arranged to meet her best friend Sue to go shopping in Bridgetown, after which the idea was to share the good news with her.

It was a very beautiful day. After shopping they headed to one of the restaurants in the largest department store in the City for lunch. Having been seated and partaking of their lunch, Sue said to Louise, "Okay now tell me about this surprise you have for me." Louise gave Sue the background regarding her new 'beau'. Sue could not contain her excitement. She jumped up from her seat, gave Louise a hug, saying," Sounds like a really great catch to me." Louise said, "Oh yes he is. The relationship has the potential to be serious. His love making is very intense, and I feel the electricity going through ever part of my body when we are 'locked' and making love, or should I say almost locked ……." Sue interjected, why? Explain to me the almost part, I don't quite understand what you are trying to say." Louise said, "Okay, first of all, do not be judgmental. When I am lying there hoping that he would finish off and 'take it', he does not. He tells me that all good things come to those who wait. And you know about my experiences - Before you could say "jack robin," all the other men that I allowed to use my body would try to achieve that objective, with the exception of Mark. As for ignorant ass Michael, within less than two hours of meeting him for the first time he was 'banging' it. Truthfully, Ray's approach sometimes frustrates me. As far as I am concern this stopping short is for the elderly, plus my love for him as of right now is very strong. I know he wants it, because it remains erect for quite some time after. I call that punishment of self."

Sue's demeanor suddenly changed. She shook her head and said, "What is the matter with you? Your problem is always to get 'banged' in a hurry. When are you going to stop that crap?" Louise responded and said, "To be honest. I want to stop being that way, but like I told you numerous times before, it is hard Sue, really very hard." Sue said," you are too complicated for me; you say repeatedly that you hate all men, you refer to them as stupid ass men, yet you want to have them on top of you in a 'flash'."

"You pretty and all of that, but most men do not stay with women who open their legs so quickly. The fact that he is taking his time is a big plus. That shows a man of great character and integrity." Louise responded and said," I guess, but secretly, I still hope that he will give me a good 'banging' soon." Sue said while frowning, "I have never and probably will never meet anyone like you. Your behavior sickens me sometimes. There are times when I swear you are bipolar."

Louise gave Sue a nasty look, and said, "You should be more sympathetic." Louise frowned, sucked her teeth. She suddenly got up from the table, signaled to the waiter that she was ready for the bill. She paid the cashier and stormed off without telling Sue goodbye.

On her way to the exit door, with her head down, she suddenly returned to the table where Sue was still sitting in amazement at what had just transpired, Louise said, "I am so sorry for my reaction just now. You are still my best friend and you will get to meet him soon." Sue responded and said, "I look forward to that. And I did not mean to be so harsh." Louise said, "You don't need to apologize, I am the problem, not you." She hugged Sue after telling her Bye.

She paid the carpark attendant and hurriedly drove home in her red sports car which incidentally was a gift from her boss. With the wind blowing through her hair, speeded along knowing that she needed enough time to 'dress up' for the dinner date with her new man. Ray arrived in a cab, at Louise's apartment at 7:00 p.m. He greeted her with a soft kiss on her lips. After they were seated in her car and were on their way, he said to her, "Wow! You look more and more beautiful every day." Reservations for dinner were made at an upscale hotel on the West Coast. After dinner, but still at the table sipping red wine, Ray looked into her eyes, held her hand said," I am in awe of your beauty. However my assessment of you is that you are a very deep, but troubled person." Louise shrugged her shoulders and did not respond." He changed the subject, and said to her," I am so smitten by you. I feel as if we are already best friends, and that is how a relationship should start, Agreed!" Louise replied softly and said, "Yes. I agree, but it does not always work that way." Ray responded and said, "Point taken, but it helps, doesn't it." She replied and said, "But of course it does."

Ray pulled his chair closer to hers, stared into her eyes, squeezed her hand tightly and said, "I have big plans for you and I. I am asking you right now to formally be my girlfriend." With a surprise look on her face, she shifted in the chair said "Gosh! I will for sure, I am so excited! I get butterflies every time I see you or think of you." He kissed her on her lips. Ray said to her, "You really know how to make me feel even happier that when we arrived for dinner." They exited the restaurant shortly after settling the bill, and walked hand in hand to Louise's vehicle. Louise drove him to his rented apartment which was on the south coast in the parish of Christ Church. He gave her a deep, long kiss prior to her departure saying, "Travel safely my love."

A week after, Sue met up with Louise at Louise's apartment. Louise filled Sue in on the dinner date, and the fact that Ray had asked her officially to be his girlfriend. However Louise was somewhat apprehensive. Sue asked her, "Why are you feeling that way? You should be the happiest person alive, with a new handsome' man, what more can a lady ask for?" Louise tried to explain, said, "My problem is that I hope the elements of my destructive pass do not come back to haunt me. You know how malicious lots of Barbadians are. You know just now they would be talking about how many men I had and more." Sue said, "I understand, just stay positive. Also maybe some day soon, when the time is right, you should tell him all about your troubled pass, that way, hearing after from any 'locals' should not make much of a difference." Louise said," I will keep that at the back of my head. It is a good idea and would save me from any embarrassment that could even ruin our relationship." She said further, "Ray is very analytical and on the whole intellectual. I am glad I made the decision to further my education, I feel very confident when communicating with him at all levels."

Louise went to the refrigerator, removed a bottle of wine. She said to Sue, "Let us drink to my success this time around, and also to you being there for me, through thick and thin." Thereafter Sue gave Louise a hug and said to her, "I leave now with much happiness for you." Louise thanked Sue for her kind sentiment and said to her, "I often wonder what I would do without you." Sue smiling exited after wishing Louise Goodbye."

The graduation ceremony for both of them took place within two weeks, and it was soon time for Ray to return to the United States of America.

Now that they had both completed their respective programs, the two had much more time for each other. They would go on week days and weekends to one of their favorite beaches. It was weekend, Saturday to be exact. They decided to go to Rockley Beach, located on the south of the island, in the parish of Christ Church. They chose a relative secluded area, lying on their beach towels. The beach was crowded with locals and visitors alike. Louise said, "This is one of the most popular beaches on the island" In amazement, Ray said, "Such a wonderful beach, blue water, and white sand. The sky is cloudless. Louise I swear I am in paradise." She said to him, oh yes, you are in paradise. That is why Barbados is called the gem of the Caribbean by most."

One Sunday evening, they drove to Cattlewash, in the North of the island, located in the parish of Saint Joseph; Ray said to her, "Wow, it's so serene and beautiful here." Louise explained to him that it was there that international surfing events had taken place. She said further, "From what I understand, it is one of the best surfing locations in the world." Ray said, "Imagine that." They then spent some time lying on the sand and frolicking in the water.

On the Monday, Louise took Ray to Brown's Beach in the parish of Saint Michael. Of course he was fascinated by the same blue water and white sand. He said, Wow! Louise, such a wonderful beach and it is also so wide." She said to him, "Oh yes it is indeed." Another popular beach that she took him too was 'Miami' Beach in the parish of Christ Church. They went for a swim and while still in the water, they locked in tight embrace, he kissed her over and over again. "She said, "Gosh! My mouth is filled with salt water, but never mind I have the 'hots' for you right now, with all of your sweet and tender kisses."

Louise said to Ray "There are other wonderful beaches on the west coast, but I would like to take you later this evening to Bottom Bay, located in the parish of Saint Philip, just before sunset." Ray said, "Thanks. I do appreciate that." She said to him, "but you must remember to bring your camera."

Ray said to her," I am so happy that our studies are over that we can relax and have so much fun in your beautiful country." Louise said to Ray, "I know that your time is running out, and it is for that reason that we are visiting places including these wonderful beaches, and if time permits we would visit other places of interest that you would not have had the opportunity to see before."

They arrived at Bottom Bay, just before sun set. The beach was quiet. Ray with camera in right hand, while holding Louise's hand they walked on the sand, but with their eyes on the sun. Finally it started to go down. Ray quickly detached from Louise. He got so excited at the specular view. He said, "When I thought Barbados could not get any better, it has." After taking several photos, he said, "So stunning, serene and romantic. All at the same time. How I love it." He then kissed her on the lips over and over again, and again.

They also visited other places of interest on the island and in some cases there was so much to 'take in', that it took the entire day. One such 'adventure' was booking space on the Safari Tour, which stopped at various places on the island that Ray had not even heard of before. Louise was so happy to be with him, she said to herself. *I truly believe that I have now found my soul mate.*

Her rendezvous with Mr. Winters had almost ceased. Louise did not want to overwhelm Mr. Winters with a sudden cessation, so gradually she became less available and less passionate about him. In any event, for Mr. Winters, the writing was already on the wall. Though he was somewhat disappointed that their relationship was falling apart, as he was now seeing less and less of her, he appeared to be happy for Louise.

Louise had earlier hinted to him that she had met someone special and that she hoped he would not take it too hard. *Besides,* Louise thought to herself, *at the end of the day, I would never be Mrs. Winters. Lots of men talk about divorcing their wives, yet they never do so. I really do not want to wait in vain and be another statistic.*

She, however, acknowledged that he was good to her and, of course, that she too was good to him. There was equity as far as she was concerned. Besides, Louise was trying really hard to give up her demons. As a result, she tried her utmost to concentrate solely on Ray, whom she knew loved her very deeply.

Chapter 23

ONE SUNDAY AFTERNOON, while lying on Brown's Beach and taking in all its beauty, including the brilliant sunset, Ray said to Louise, "Barbados is indeed a beautiful and wonderful paradise. This is the land that I would love for us to retire in when we grow old. I have some big plans for both of us." Louise listened intently. Ray said to Louise, "I want for you to come to America with me. I leave here in a month." Louise was happy to hear that but wanted more details with regard to her ability to stay in the United States, given the fact that she only had a visitor's visa. Ray told her that that was the least of their problems. He also explained to her that she could get a student's visa in the interim to do graduate studies, and once she was enrolled at a university, she would have no problem as he would take care of her financially. Ray also said that he had discussed with his Dad the signing of the Guarantor Form for her student visa and that his Dad had agreed to do so. In a very short span of time, Louise obtained her student visa.

Two weeks later Louise prepared her letter of resignation, and by 10:00 a.m. that Monday morning she knocked on Mr. Winter's officer door, entered and said to him, "Good Morning boss. How are you?" With a broad smile on his face, he responded and said, fine, now that you are here with me." She remained standing. He got up and gave her a kiss on the lips, then asked her, "And what do you have for me today my darling? Yourself right. Louise a bit nervous, gave a faint smile, said, "Boss we will see about the giving later." She then said to him rather quickly, "I did mention to you some time ago that I might be leaving and here, this is my official letter of resignation." Mr. Winters appeared shock, stepped back, mouth open, while he stared at the contents of the letter. He said, "Yes! but I did not realize it would be coming so soon."

He quickly regained his composure, said "I am happy for you. Louise! Honestly, you are one of the nicest persons I have ever met, personally and otherwise. It will be very difficult to replace you". She responded, "Thanks for your kind sentiments." He moved closer to her, embraced her, and planted a kiss on her lips which to her seemed so 'hollow' at this stage. He then placed one hand on her butt." She was very upset and said to herself, *"Is he for real. Am I his property, I think not.* She then slowly pulled away. She then wished him, Good Bye, exited and closed the door behind her.

One week later after bidding her mother, siblings, and best friend Sue good-bye, Louise and Ray arrived in Massachusetts, where Louise was set to do Graduate Studies in Human Resource Management at one of the Universities of her choice. Meanwhile, Ray went back to work with his company but now worked in a higher capacity. He looked after Louise's every need, financially and otherwise.

Chapter 24

ONE EVENING WHILE watching television and eating popcorn, with Ray's body stretched out on the sofa and Louise partially lying on him; Ray surprised Louise by asking her to tell him about her life. He said, "Louise, there are times when you look so very sad. I wish for the day when I can see more happiness on your face. Please open up to me and tell me your story."

Louise felt the pressure rising in her head. At first she denied that there were issues, but Ray persisted. After the constant prodding, Louise broke down and tearfully told him all about her troubled childhood and how it had impacted totally on the very poor choices she made in life as a result.

She explained how she never knew her father and was sad and depressed as a child growing up most of the time due to this situation. How she was sexually molested for a period of time when she was a preteen and beyond, by an older man who was involved with her mother and whom she ultimately made paid her for sex. Louise admitted to Ray also more about her dark past as a young adult, whereby she became a nymphomaniac, and how her self-esteem had been very low and remained low from the time she was sexually molested.

She also told him that many times after having sex with some of these various men with no love in her heart for any of them, when she showered, she would scrub her skin with a scrubbing brush with so much intensity, that parts became bruised and bled. That in her mind she felt that she was actually trying to scrub the filth away. She said further, "Ironically, I was so messed up that I felt that having sex with all of them, to me, was like 'pay back' time, and that as far as I was concerned, most of them, if not all were a bunch of 'stupid ass men', whom I took pleasure in having sex with, at least once, maybe twice. But when they felt that they were 'getting somewhere" as far as the relationship, I took pride in telling them to get to hell out of my life; and when I saw the pitiful look on their faces, and the begging as a result of rejection by me, it gave me a feeling of euphoria and power." She added, "but there were also many 'one night stands' too."

Nothing was omitted. She sobbed uncontrollably in between. Ray comforted Louise and explained to her that none of that mattered anymore—that the person who sexually molested her and trigged the occurrences that followed, should have been punished and that he would be there for her forever.

Furthermore, Ray said to her, "Louise, I want to marry you. Will you marry me?" Louise was somewhat surprised by this news and she was unable to respond right away. She placed her arms around him and told him while sobbing softly, "Yes, I will."

They decided on a small wedding as Ray said that huge weddings were a waste of money. He quickly added, "But, Louise, the decision is also yours. She agreed. They had a small church wedding, with guests of mainly Ray's family. Her gown was an awesome designer gown in ivory, with an amazing tiara.

Prior to leaving Barbados, Louise had already informed Ray of her previous marriage. She did not, however, explain at that time that she was not sure if she could have kids. She now felt so secure in this relationship that she did indicate to him that there was a possibility that she might not be able to bear him any children. That she sadly had numerous terminations. He acknowledged that the situation with the terminations was unfortunate. However, he reassured her that she will not be judged by that situation, and as far as their relationship was concerned, there was no conditional love, that he loved her unconditionally and that he would always be there for her.

But there was one thing he asked Louise to promise him. He said to her, "Louise, I want you to try really hard and erase the hatred you have for men from your thoughts. It is unhealthy. Do not allow bad men to cloud your judgment and cause you to be unhappy. Remove the shackles, please." He explained to her further that there are good women and bad women; so too, there are good men and bad men. He urged her to look at life from a different perspective. He said, "Louise, you deserve the best, and I will give you nothing but the best." He reiterated, "I will love you forever and ever. As we both age, the feelings would continue to grow stronger and stronger. God has been good to me. I am truly blessed to have you in my life."

Of course, Ray recognized that Louise's problems and hatred toward men had persisted because she lacked the counseling she deserved, and that she should have spoken to someone in authority about the traumatic events regarding her sexual abuse in particular. Ray said to her that none of that mattered now, that she must wipe the slate clean; and that today was the first day of the rest of her life.

Louise was amazed and very happy at the same time that she had not only found true happiness but that she had found someone whom she loved deeply and knew that he felt the same way. She was now beginning to really see the light at the end of the tunnel. She thanked God for sending Ray into her life. This was now the first time in her life that she genuinely without reservations cared for a male—that male miraculously was her husband now. Their lovemaking was extremely intense. She had never before experienced such warmth and joy from any other man. She felt so complete and special now. Actually, she just loved herself more and more every day, and Ray constantly reassured her of her strengths.

There were no longer any thoughts of even Mr. Winters. In fact, Louise felt that he too had exploited her like all the other men that came into her life, with the exception of Mark. She tried hard not to start counting these men because she knew the number of men that she had slept with in her comparatively short life would be mind-boggling to many. She also remembered what Ray had told her about erasing the past, and that was exactly what Louise resolved that she would do, and that she did.

Her life was now so complete that there were times when it even appeared surreal to her, and she swore that she must be dreaming. Louise loved the part of Massachusetts were they resided. In fact, she especially loved Boston. There were so many young college students around at the various Universities that Louise, though a bit older than most, felt youthful. This feeling was a far cry from what she had experienced when she was younger in Barbados. Louise even surprised herself that she took to the snow and really liked it when it had just fallen, especially when she looked across at the park from the ten story apartment where they lived, and watched the beautiful white snow as it fell.

On weekends they visited places of interest in Massachusetts. Those places included The Museum of Science, The New England Aquarium, and The Boston Common.

They were so much in love that they showed public affection and their deep love for each other, wherever they went. They could be seen holding hands, in tight embrace, and kissing each other over and over, impulsively with total abandon! During such a show of love for each other, one day, while walking in the park, Ray reminded Louise and said, "There is no greater love than ours. We will be together forever", Louise nodded her head in agreement.

One night, lying in bed, facing each other, stroking her hair, he pulled her closer to him, he tore off her negligee, slowly kissed her all over her body, telling her again and again that his love for her was intense and indescribable; she attempted to respond. He placed his finger on her lips and was on top of her, slowly entering into her. After it was done, they both fell asleep with their bodies interlocked as one.

Louise completed her graduate studies and performed exceptionally well. She made the dean's list. Ray continued to shower her with love, affection and attention and told her that he was very proud of her accomplishments. Louise succeeded in getting a well-paying job at one of the larger insurance companies as Human Resource Director. She now also had her residence status as Ray's wife and was delighted.

They obviously never used protection during their lovemaking, but no baby appeared to be coming their way. Louise was still hopeful that she would bear Ray a son or a daughter as, in her words, she was getting older, and the longer it took, the more the likelihood that she would not conceive. One day she asked Ray if he was disappointed that it had not happened after four years of marriage. Ray looked at her and said relatively sternly but tenderly, "Absolutely not! What will be, will be. God gave you to me, and you are the most precious gift I have and will ever have. If he does not see it fit to grant us a child, I am still forever grateful and happy that I have met you. Our lives are complete with or without a child. My love, please stop worrying. Always remember these words I will always love you forever unconditionally regardless of the circumstance.

Chapter 25

THE YEARS WENT by rather quickly, or so it seemed. There was never an occasion when either of the two went to bed angry at the other. It was the perfect marriage. They were both healthy individuals who went walking in the park, and when not too busy with work, found time to work out in the gym.

Ray got another promotion in his organization and could not contain his excitement. When he arrived home and both were having dinner, he shared the news with Louise, who was ecstatic. The new assignment was hectic and demanding, but Ray managed well.

Louise utilized some of her salary on a monthly basis and sent it to her mother back in Barbados. Even her mother's skin tone was now more refined, and her attire was often the envy of many in the village. Louise not only outfitted her mother, but all her siblings now benefited from the US dollars that Louise sent back home. Louise also had their old wooden home completely reconstructed into a stone house. She had done so well financially that she was also able to purchase, along with a smaller contribution from Ray, a piece of land back home in Barbados for Ray and herself. Ray offered to contribute half of the cost, but Louise kept reminding him of her huge student debt that he had paid off entirely on his own, and that she would have none of it. Louise always liked the south coast of the island.

The land was located in one of the heights/ terraces on the south coast of Barbados and had a beautiful view looking on to the sea. Ray's contribution, however, helped in finalizing the sale. They were able to pay off the land very quickly and commenced the construction of a home, which they called their dream home. They had hired a reliable contractor, but depended on her mother Naomi, and brother Oswald to pay frequent visits, as they had heard of other projects which were long and drawn out on the island, particularly when the owners lived overseas. In addition, they wanted to ensure that the home was not only built to their specifications but constructed to withstand high winds.

Barbados has never had a major hurricane since Hurricane Janet in 1955, but the vulnerability is always there as it is located in the hurricane zone, being part of the Caribbean Island chain.

It took just under ten months for the construction of their dream home to complete. Upon its completion, they both took a two-week vacation leave from their respective jobs to Barbados. All the furnishings for their dream home were shipped to Barbados ahead of their arrival. Although not necessary, as Louise had acquired a very sophisticated taste over the years, they hired an interior decorator in advance. Even most of the flower gardens were in full bloom.

As the airline touched down at the Grantley Adams International Airport, Louise said to Ray, "Gosh I am getting very emotional. So many good things have happened to me since I was last home." He said to her "I am overjoyed to be back here." Louise's mother, siblings and her best friend Sue were all there to meet them. Louise greeted her family, giving each a big hug. Louise held on to her mother's outstretched arms, telling her mother, "I love you so very much.

Throughout all of my drama and tribulation, I knew you carried a huge burden on your back, worrying about me." Naomi, being a very emotional person, shook her head in the affirmative and shed a tear, while holding on to Louise very tightly.

With a look of admiration on her face, she complimented each of her siblings, one by one. Avonda said to her "We give thanks to you for all that you have been sending. Everyone in our village talking about us, about how well-groomed and well-dressed we always are." Louise smiling responded, "That is so nice. I love it." Louise turned to Fred and Peter and said, "I understand that you all have totally given up your demons, and are now gainfully employed on a steady basis." They both literally said in tandem, "Oh Yes, we have. With a beautiful loving sister like you, we had no choice, and of course John, Oswald's friend set our complete turn around in motion." Louise then reached out to Oswald, she gave him another big hug while saying, "And look at my big brother, you are not looking bad yourself either." Oswald responded, "Thanks for everything 'lil sis'. I am overjoyed to see you."

Louise then turned to her dear friend Sue, with both hands out stretched, gave her a huge hug, while saying, "Gosh! I have saved the best for last. My dearest friend forever."

Sue responded, "Look at you! You still look as young as ever. Wow!" Louise stopped briefly, smiled radiantly while she posed, and spun around saying, "I am forever young."

Louise then said to Sue, "Come let me reintroduce you to the love of my life". During the reintroduction, Sue said to Ray, "Very nice to meet you again. See that! Your wife gets married twice and me, I cannot even get it once." Louise, laughing out loudly said to Sue, "Your time will come, maybe a priest will marry you." Ray said to the entire family, "I am delighted to be back in Barbados. The best part was meeting my soul mate." Naomi responded and said, "That is so true. You all are a perfect match." Louise chimed in and said, "I know, everyone says that about us. Amazing isn't it." With the initial pleasantry completed, Naomi said to Louise, "I know you all are in a great hurry to see your beautiful home tomorrow, but I am inviting you all to have lunch with us as a family prior." Louise said, "Oh yes, we will be there." They then departed in the taxi which took them to the hotel after waving goodbye to her family and friend."

The next day Ray suggested that Louise go to the luncheon with her family alone as he was feeling a bit 'under the weather'; but that he should feel better later, for them to travel to their dream home". He reminded her about the collection of the vehicle from the car rental company prior. She nodded her head in the affirmative. Louise kissed him before departing to her mother's place in a taxi, blew him another kiss, smiled while saying, "Get some more rest, my prince in shinning Armor. See you later."

On arrival at her mother's place, Louise was enamored on seeing the huge 'Welcome Home Louise' decorative sign on the front door. More hugs from her mother and siblings were the 'order of the day'. The main dish consisted of green peas and rice, macaroni pie, pork chops, steam pudding and souse, flying fish, and beef stew, along with tossed salad. For desert, apart from fruit salad, there was also 'Bajan coconut Bread'.

Prior to her departure by taxi, Louise again hugged her mother and each of her siblings.

On arrival back to the hotel, Ray informed Louise that when she was gone, the vehicle was delivered to the hotel. She was also happy to know that he was feeling better.

They arrived at their dream home at approximately 3:30 p.m. Louise could not contain her excitement, and she had not even entered at that point. They perused the kitchen. She said to Ray, "I like the size of our kitchen, so spacious, oh how I love it." She looked at Ray and said, "Aren't you excited?" He responded and said to her, "Of course I am." Suddenly he lifted her up, placed her on the kitchen counter. He was so excited he peeled off her clothing, and dropped them on the floor. He kissed her ravenously, he also fondled her breasts and of course her vagina. He said to her "My darling, right in this house, we will retire years from now". She was enjoying the foreplay so very much, she did not respond.

He quickly lifted her down, while still kissing her, with hands all over her naked body, lead her up the stairs to the Master Bedroom, placed her on the bed and was on top of her while looking into her eyes with a smile on his face, said, "What an awesome way to christen our new home." Louise laughed softly and said "Of course my love, awesome indeed." Shortly thereafter, as if in a hypnotic state, she continued to repeat, "My love! My love! Within minutes she screamed. He continued for a while longer until he too reached his plateau.

The two weeks in Barbados were going by quickly. It was almost time to go back to Massachusetts. Of course, they were able to visit a number of places of interest on the island. Places that Ray did not have the opportunity to visit while studying in Barbados. Ray was particularly impressed with Harrison's Cave, in the parish of Saint Thomas, the Animal Flower Cave, in the parish of Saint Lucy, and George Washington House in the parish of Saint Michael, especially after the tour guide explained the facts surrounding this house; he was then able to understand why it was called George Washington House. Being a patriotic American, he felt proud and was pleasantly surprised to know that the first President of his country had actually resided in this handsome Georgian-style two-story house. The fact that Barbados was the only place that George Washington ever visited outside of America was truly fascinating to him.

Other activities that interested him greatly were the Atlantis submarine and the MPV *Harbor Master*, a boat that took tourists and locals alike on a scenic tour mainly on the west coast. It was the first time that Ray really experienced the infectious music of calypso. He was also intrigued with 'Mother Sally', of which he had seen the enactment when he went to the Bajan Roots & Rhythms dinner show, which was staged at the Plantation Garden Theatre in the parish of Christ Church. Louise explained to Ray that Mother Sally was one of the Bajan folk characters. Ray found the exaggerated back end of this character to be quite hilarious.

As for the Oistin's Fish Fry on Friday nights, he had never seen such a beautiful setting with music, dancing, and the aroma of fried fish and other sumptuous Barbadian delicacies. He did enjoy the steel band music tremendously, which was being played that night. Another tour that Ray found interesting and enlightening was the visit to Saint Nicholas Abbey, which is located in the parish of Saint

Peter. Ray also enjoyed very much his tour on the west coast of Barbados, in Saint James and again on the east coast, Bathsheba, in the parish of Saint Joseph. He observed that their contrast with the south coast was quite stark, especially Bathsheba.

The night prior to their departure, Louise 'the kind soul' she is, organized a house warming party at their new home. Guests included residences in the village where she grew up. The village priest from her childhood was present to bless the home and even some persons from the village who at times were not very kind to her as a child, because of her differences in features and looks in general were now very happy to be part of the gathering. She remembered what Ray had told her on many occasions, so she now held no malice towards these people. In fact she embraced them all in the process, thanking them for being part of Ray's and her celebration.

The day had arrived for them to return to the United States. As they left Barbados, it was with a tinge of nostalgia for both of them to leave this beautiful island. Those thoughts quickly disappeared as they knew that they now owned a piece of the 'rock', and at the right time, they would be retiring there.

Chapter 26

RAY AND LOUISE quickly settled back in to the routine of work, exercise, and the occasional movie at a theatre in the area where they lived.

Ray's schedule at work was becoming more intense. Very often he would work for as many as twelve hours a day and, sometimes, even a bit longer. Louise would always ensure that his dinner was ready, that there were always clean towels, and in general, that everything was in place for him by the time he arrived home. Despite the long hours, Ray always came through the door with a smile on his face. Louise would say to him, "You look so happy, like you now ready to start work." Ray would always kiss his wife on her lips before they both departed for their respective jobs, and he would also always kiss her on his arrival home. On one occasion on his arrival home after the usual long hours at work Ray said to Louise, after she as usual marveled at his smile and general upbeat demeanor "I am happy because I have arrived home to my lovely wife, and my darling, nothing makes me happier than when I see your beautiful and charming face. You have given me so much joy you will never know how much you mean to me."

Shortly thereafter his demeanor change and he had a serious look on his face, and in a softer tone of voice, he said, "But, Louise, I am not sure, but there is so much pressure at my work place that I am getting these headaches that sometimes last for a short while but sometimes for a long period. I never told you before, as I do not want you to worry unnecessarily. I believe it could be my schedule, but you know me, I have to give my job my all, and that is all I know. When the headaches start, I just ignore them and take some painkillers in between." Louise looked at him, a bit concerned, and said, "But, Ray, you probably need to slow down. You are overworked and stressed, that's why you might be getting these headaches, and you are not letting me in on what is going on." Ray responded, "But, Louise, it is nothing to worry about, so please do not worry, Okay?" She questioned Ray further about the headaches. He explained to her that the headaches were usually worse in the morning than in the afternoon. After further prodding, he told her that there were times when the headaches occurred wherein he felt nausea. At one point, they both concluded that these headaches might be migraine related.

Several weeks passed by, and Ray was still getting the headaches. He was now getting some loss of movement in his left arm. He was, however, thankful that it was not occurring in his right arm, which would have restricted him more, being right-handed. When they did go out at night, which was now only occasionally because of his condition, Ray would ask Louise to do the driving as his vision had diminished somewhat.

Louise's alarm came when she realized that Ray was having some speech difficulty. Louise had urged Ray in recent times to go to the doctor, but like several males, he had not done so. Given the fact that he had not done so, and with other situations occurring, Louise insisted that he must go. "Ray, I know you do not like going to the doctor, but I have made arrangements for you to have an MRI performed to see what is really going on with you.

By now your headaches should have ceased, but rather than cease, you are now having additional problems. I really want you to have it done urgently, my darling. I will be there with you, Okay!

Furthermore, if you love me as much as you have always said you do, prove it to me now by having the test done.

You must realize that if you are not well, I am not well either because my stress levels are increasing with my worry about you." Ray agreed to have the test done. However, on the scheduled day, Ray declared that he was feeling much better and that he did not need to see a doctor and that, furthermore, why was she so obsessed with him seeing a doctor? He said, "Doctor! I am not going to any doctor. I am fine."

Chapter 27

MEANWHILE, LOUISE HAD received a call from the Vice President in Ray's department, who expressed concerns with regard to Ray's change of behavior. His Vice President also tried to talk him into going to a physician, but Ray literally went ballistic. There was now a complete change in Ray's behavior. It was as if he were a different person altogether. His behavior at work had started to affect his ability to produce at the standard he had set and that had allowed him to reach the point he had in the organization.

Louise became irate. Ray had also developed a don't-care attitude, and anyone who talked about his erratic behavior got a tongue-lashing from him.

One day, Louise was at her lunch break when she got an urgent call that she should come to Ray's office immediately. As Louise drove as fast as the speed limit would allow to Ray's office, all sorts of crazy thoughts were now going through her head. Louise started to pray, "Dear God, please heal Ray, whatever the affliction. I so much want my normal Ray back in my life. Please give Ray the wisdom to understand that he really needs help urgently."

Finally, upon her arrival in the car park of his office, she hurriedly slammed the door of her vehicle, even forgetting to lock it. She tried waiting for the elevator but concluded that it was far better if she ran up the flight of stairs leading to the fifth floor, where Ray's department was located.

When she reached there, out of breath and barely able to speak, she was greeted by the secretary, who told her that they had to call an ambulance for Ray as he had literally passed out. The secretary told her that a message was left on her phone after the initial call to her to let her know that Ray was taken by ambulance to the hospital as they could not wait any longer for her arrival due to his state, and as time was of the essence, a decision was made to get an ambulance right away.

Luckily, the hospital was not too far away. Louise rushed backed down the five flights of stairs and headed to the hospital where Ray was taken. On her arrival, she found that Ray was hooked up to several drips. He also had an oxygen mask on his face to facilitate his breathing.

The nurse in charge greeted her, and then referred her to the doctor overseeing Ray's condition. The doctor explained to Louise the condition that Ray had arrived in. He said that Ray was semiconscious and that the vital signs, though irregular and weak, were still intact. Arrangements were made for magnetic resonance imaging (MRI) to be done the very next day.

Louise remained overnight at the hospital to be at Ray's bedside. She held his hand and kissed him on the forehead, whispering to him how much she loved him and how she prayed that the problem was not a serious one. She was not sure if Ray recognized her presence. Louise was so exhausted from the events of the day that she fell into a deep sleep momentarily, only to be awakened in the early hours of the morning by Ray moaning and vomiting uncontrollably. She rang the alarm bell, and within minutes, the nurse in charge appeared.

The doctor was called, and he instructed the nurse to set up an anti-vomit drip as Ray was still unable to take any medication orally.

The MRI was done later that day. By then, Ray had opened his eyes and acknowledged the presence of his still-beautiful but anxious wife. He gave a faint smile and then closed his eyes again.

The results took approximately twenty-four hours. Even though the doctor had some idea as to what was happening, he awaited the official results from the radiologist, which he subsequently received and Ray remained hospitalized. Louise met with the doctor at a prearranged time. The doctor greeted Louise while telling her that she was a very strong woman and, given the short span of time that he had met her, that he also recognized that she loved and cared for her husband very deeply. Louise just nodded her head, hoping that the doctor would swiftly tell her about the findings. *Is he preparing me for the worst?* She silently said to herself.

The doctor explained all the images in medical terminology. At the end of the process, he finally told Louise that Ray had a brain tumor and that it was located in a very difficult section of the brain. The part that caused her to break down and cry was when the doctor told her that it was cancerous and that it was a very aggressive tumor and that the prognosis was very grim. Her body went limp as she slumped over.

She eventually left the doctor's office about an hour after being comforted by both the doctor and the nurse. Everything felt surreal to her. How could it be that the man she loved so dearly, the man who gave her solace, the man who was able to reverse the low self-esteem/image she had of herself after those terrible events in her past, that man who loved her unconditionally—how could he be so ill right now? Louise was not sure how she managed to get back to her car. She literally felt that she was walking on air and that it was all a terrible dream.

The months that followed were very difficult for her as she watched Ray deteriorate at quite a rapid pace.

Ray passed away six months after his initial hospitalization. Louise was inconsolable. There was no viewing of the body on the day of the wake. Louise would not allow anyone to see Ray in that condition. Certainly not her Ray. During the ceremony, many people attested to the kind, gentle, and honorable man named Raymond Hill, and they were grateful that he had touched their lives in one way or another. The young and the old all shared the same depth of sadness at his passing. Condolences poured in from persons she knew and from persons that she did not know. The burial took place the morning after the wake.

Chapter 28

I T WAS NOW almost a year since Ray had passed away. Louise had secured her citizenship but was still in the same state of grief that she was on the day he passed. There were times when her mind would play tricks on her. She sometimes swore that she heard Ray's voice talking to her telling her how much he loved her. Other times she was sure he was lying in bed, right beside her, cuddling her while telling her that everything was okay and that it was just a bad dream.

Shortly thereafter, at home and all alone lying on her bed she said to herself aloud, while wiping the tears from her eyes, *"I can't remain in this country any longer, the pain of not having the love of my life here with me is too great."*

The next day Louise resigned her job and made reservations for a one way flight back too Barbados.

Two weeks later she arrived in Barbados. She collected from the airport the rental car which she reserved prior to her arrival. She drove to their newly constructed home.

Louise had been on tranquilizers since Ray's passing. Sadly, she had been increasing the dosage with much frequency. She walked up the stairs to the master bedroom just staring up at the ceiling with a blank expression on her face. That blank expression on her face went on nonstop for approximately two weeks since her arrival. She would also only get a snack to sustain her, and mainly drank water. She rarely took a bath, wore the same house dress, hair remained unkempt, and basically looked like a zombie. She spoke to no one, not even her mother and other siblings were aware that she had returned to Barbados.

It was the beginning of the third week. She dragged herself up from the bed and is on the phone, teary eyed still in an unkempt and zombie state. She called her best friend Sue, she is barely audible said, "Hello Sue, it is me Louise." Sue said to her, "I can barely understand what you are saying. "My condolences to you again. How are you doing?" She responded, "Not good at all! I am here in Barbados." Sue very surprise said, "What? You are! You did not tell me that you were coming home. When did you arrive and how long will you be here?" Louise responded, "A few weeks ago and for good. I could not stay in America without my Ray. I just can't take this emptiness I am feeling from not having him at my side."

Sue tried to comfort her, said, "Time Louise. Only time will help you. I feel so badly for you. Everything happened so fast, and so suddenly. I am still in a state of shock, but I know I could never feel the way you do, so I will not tell you that I know how you are feeling; but I will be there for you forever."

Louise wiped the tears from her eyes which streamed down her face. Spoke slowly, and in a measured tone said, "If only I were able to bear a child for Ray, I know the pain would have been lessened. I wonder why me? When I think of all of those pregnancies which I terminated, and the numerous men that I have slept with that I loss count of, all of those things are haunting me now. I am praying that I will maintain my sanity." Sue responded, "You will. But time Louise, trust me. As the bible says, it is the only healer."

Louise responded, "Honestly, I really am not sure if or when I will heal. I wish I had lived a better life and not allow this human frailty. I just do not understand how it is that God gave me the opportunity to reproduce on so many occasions, and me, awful me destroying life on each occasion. I have committed the ultimate sin.

And now without the love of my life, I think God is punishing me now." Sue offered more comforting words said, "Oh please! Please do not 'beat up' on yourself like that. God is a forgiving God, he says he will never forsake us, and he will never forsake you. Can I come over and spend some time with you for as long as necessary? I don't like how you are sounding. Remember the good times we spent together, Please say yes!"

Louise responded, "No thanks" She hesitated for a moment, and then said, "I guess I will be alright and bye for now." Sue was not prepared to give up, responded "Are you sure you will be alright?" Louise in a very soft tone of voice said "I really can't say, but thanks and bye." Sue became extremely worried, said, "Bye for now, Love You."

Sue was visibly distraught. After the conversation with tears settled in her eyes, she shook her head from side to side and said to herself, Oh! *How I wish she would 'let me in'.* Sue reflected on the Louise she knew, her personality, witty and funny, but at the same time complicated.

Two days later, evening time, Louise drove slowly to Bottom Bay, one of Ray's favorite beaches on the island. Sunset was approaching, a truly magnificent view at Bottom Bay as the sun sets. The beach was basically deserted. She got out of the vehicle with purse in one hand and bottle water in the other. She looked towards the beautiful ocean momentarily. Then turned around while continuing to wipe away the tears which were streaming down her face, she said aloud to herself, *"Ray my darling! I so wish that you were here with me." You were the love of my life. This pain is too much for me to endure. If only I could turn back the hands of time."*

Suddenly, she opened her purse 'popped' a hand full of her tranquilizers into her mouth, drank the water, then sobbing and screaming loudly and uncontrollably to the top of her voice said," *Oh God! Why me!! Why me!!* She becomes exhausted, lays down rolling over and over on the sand still screaming (like an echo) said again and again, *God! Please forgive me!! Please forgive me!!* She momentarily holds her stomach as if in anguish and pain, vomited persistently, until she lies absolutely silent not breathing and all alone!

"The author does a good job of presenting realistic dialogue that reflects the actual sound and inflection of her characters. The book *Growing Up in Barbados* is a brave story of a young woman's journey through life. It's a quick and engaging read that is likely to appeal to readers who enjoy realistic accounts, culture and history, and strong, complicated female protagonists"

—Romance Reviewed by: Gillian Pemberton, Pacific Book Review Express (W/ Pacific Book Awards)